LOST AND FOUND

LOST AND FOUND

Andrew Clements

Illustrations by Mark Elliott

SCHOLASTIC INC.
New York Toronto London Auckland Sydney
Mexico City New Delhi Hong Kong Buenos Aires

Also by Andrew Clements

No Talking
Dogku
Room One
A Million Dots
Lunch Money
The Last Holiday Concert
The Report Card
A Week in the Woods
The Jacket
The School Story
The Janitor's Boy
The Landry News
Frindle
Jake Drake, Bully Buster
Jake Drake, Know-It-All
Jake Drake, Teacher's Pet
Jake Drake, Class Clown

ISBN-13: 978-0-545-13828-4
ISBN-10: 0-545-13828-0

12 11 10 9 8 7 6 5 4 3 2 1   9 10 11 12 13 14/0

Printed in the U.S.A.   23

First Scholastic printing, January 2009

Book design by Cara Petrus
The text for this book is set in Bembo.
The illustrations for this book are rendered in pencil.

For Douglas and Roselyn Paul, dear friends

LOST AND FOUND

ALPHABETICAL

J ay Grayson was twelve years old, so the first day of school shouldn't have felt like such a big deal. But when he turned the corner onto Baker Street and saw the long brick building, he had to force himself to keep walking toward it. And Jay knew exactly why he felt so tensed up on this Tuesday morning in September: He was a new kid at a new school in a new town. Plus, his brother had stayed home sick today, so there wouldn't be even one familiar face in the whole school. He had to deal with this first day of sixth grade all on his own.

Jay's mom had offered to come to school and help get him checked in. "I'm not some little baby, Mom." That's what he had told her. Which was true.

So as he walked through the front doors of Taft Elementary School with a small crowd of other

kids, Jay tried to look on the bright side. He told himself, *This could be a lot worse.*

And by that, Jay meant that it could have been like nine months ago when his family had moved to Denver, Colorado, in the middle of January. Jumping into a new school halfway through fifth grade? Miserable. By comparison, this most recent move to Clifton, Ohio, had worked out a lot better— they'd gotten settled into their new house exactly one day before the start of the school year.

Clifton seemed like a nice enough place to live. Their neighborhood was just outside the Cleveland city limits. Jay's brother had complained that the town seemed a little worn out, a little run-down. But that was what their dad had liked about it. "You should always buy a house in a neighborhood that's got some room for improvement," he said.

And Mom had said, "It'll be all right for a while. And who knows? Maybe in a year or two we'll move to a bigger home in a nicer area."

Jay's parents were working for an insurance company in Cleveland. And having them both gone all day was a new development. Before, his mom had worked part-time during school hours. This year both parents were going to be putting in a full day. Coming home to an empty house after school would be different, but the plan was that the two brothers would always come home together, and Mom and Dad would be there by dinnertime. And their office was only fifteen minutes away.

As long as the whole family could be together under one roof at the end of the day, Jay didn't much care where they lived, and their new neighborhood seemed fine to him.

The school looked okay too. They had driven past the place yesterday afternoon. And the best part? Taft Elementary was only three blocks from their house. That meant no bus riding, no waiting in lines before and after school. Being a walker was the way to go. And on this cool September morning, the walk had taken Jay exactly twelve minutes, door to door.

Once he got beyond the entryway of the school, Jay began looking for his homeroom. He followed the signs to the sixth-grade hall, and a big banner on his right announced, IF YOU'RE IN GRADE SIX, AND YOUR LAST NAME STARTS WITH A THROUGH L, THEN THIS IS YOUR HOMEROOM! There was one other sixth-grade homeroom for all the kids whose names began with the letters *M* through *Z*.

Jay found his name on a slip of paper taped to a

desk, so he shrugged off his book bag, sat down, and then watched his new homeroom teacher as she bustled around the room. Mrs. Lane—that was the name written in perfect cursive on the chalkboard. She seemed nice enough. Not too old, not too young. Not too stiff, not too perky. And as she talked with some kids, Jay decided that her voice was easy to listen to. Not too sharp, not too sweet.

Jay looked around and discovered that Mrs. Lane's room was jammed with books. There were bins of books on every windowsill, bookcases along every wall, and there was a reading corner where the cushions and beanbag chairs were flanked by a pair of wide bookshelves that started at the floor and went almost to the ceiling. Jay wouldn't have described himself as a bookworm, but he was always in the middle of a book, sometimes two or three. So the room looked good to him.

He felt a tap on his shoulder, and when he turned around, the guy behind him smiled and said, "I saw the name on your desk. You're Jay, right?"

Jay smiled back and nodded. "Right." The kid had broad shoulders, bright blond hair, and the bluest eyes Jay had ever seen up close.

He said, "I'm Alex. You weren't here last year, were you?"

Jay shook his head. "We just moved to town—like, yesterday. From Colorado."

The kid kept smiling, and Jay saw that one of his front teeth was half broken off. It was a jagged break, and it made his whole mouth look crooked.

He noticed Jay staring and said, "It broke off during a hockey game. And my mom says there's no point getting it fixed until I quit playing hockey. Except that's never gonna happen. The guys on the team call me Fang," and Alex shaped his lips so only his two front teeth were showing. Jay decided it was a good nickname.

Jay wanted to ask him where the ice rink was, but the bell rang, and right away the principal's voice came over the intercom. She welcomed everyone, then made four or five announcements, and then led the Pledge of Allegiance.

The intercom went silent, and the teacher looked around the room and smiled. "As a lot of you know, I'm Mrs. Lane, and I'm glad to see all of you this morning. You're sixth graders now, so that makes you the big kids here at Taft Elementary. The other sixth-grade teachers and I are going to do our best to get you ready to move on to junior high, and this is going to be a great year for all of us. Now, you've each found your own desk, and until

I've learned everyone's name, I want you to use that same seat every morning. Right after the Pledge of Allegiance we'll start promptly with attendance, because homeroom is only eight minutes long. So when I call your name, please raise your hand and say, 'Present.'"

The teacher looked at her seating chart and then said, "Sarah Alton?"

"Present."

"Tanya Atwater?"

"Present."

"Ryan Bateman?"

"Present."

"Kelly Bellamy?"

"Present."

Mrs. Lane kept plowing ahead through the alphabet, and after eleven more names, she said, "Jay Grayson?"

And he said, "Present."

Then the teacher said, "Alex Grellman?"

And Alex, sitting right behind him, said, "Present."

Jay Grayson sat straight up in his chair, and then he almost raised his hand. Because Mrs. Lane had made a mistake. She had definitely made a mistake. She hadn't called his brother's name.

Because whenever the attendance was called off alphabetically like this, the teacher *always* said, "Jay Grayson" and then, "Ray Grayson." Every time, it was Jay first, and then Ray. Always.

Because Jay and Ray weren't just brothers. Jay and Ray were twins.

CHAPTER 2

ONE, TWO

The boys had been born six minutes apart—Grayson baby one, and Grayson baby two. Some twins look a little alike, and some twins look a lot alike, and some twins don't look alike at all. But some twins look *exactly* alike. They look like two peas in a pod, two ducks on a pond, two spoons in a drawer. And Grayson baby one and Grayson baby two were *that* sort of twins, completely identical—all except for one tiny, faint freckle on the ankle of baby number one.

Sue and Jim Grayson were the mom and dad, and they thought it was great to get two kids at once. Their family doubled in one day. And when the babies turned out to be boys, that was great too—although both Sue and Jim had secretly hoped for one of each, a boy and a girl. But each child was born healthy and strong, and that was all that really mattered. And the new parents were completely happy.

In fact, they were so happy that they were also a little giddy, maybe a bit dizzy, sort of the way it feels after riding a roller coaster. And as they sat together two hours after the boys were born, each one holding a child, both parents began giggling and grinning about how wonderful it was to have two beautiful sons.

Then a nurse walked into the room and said, "Have you decided on their names? No? Well you need to do that before you leave the hospital. So the sooner the better."

The parents giggled and grinned and giggled some more as they tried out name after name after name after name. And the boys looked so similar that Sue and Jim couldn't resist giving them similar names. And two hours later they each signed both birth certificates. Baby number one was named Ray, and baby number two was named Jay. And Ray's middle name was Jay, and Jay's middle name was Ray. Less than five hours into their first day, the boys became Ray Jay and Jay Ray, the Grayson twins.

The picture-taking frenzy started the moment the twins got home from the hospital. Both pairs of grandparents were waiting, and all four of them went nuts. Granny Grayson said, "Can you *believe* how *kee-yoot* these two teeny-tiny sweet patooties are? They are just the *yummiest* little things. There, hold 'em up together, over that way, closer to the window. So I can see both their faces. Can you get 'em to smile at the same time?" *Click, click, click.*

Sue's mom, Gramma Herndon, said, "Here, let's get these old white hospital blankets off of my precious baby boys. And let's put these nice new blue blankies around them, one for each. There—isn't that better? Now, Susie, you hold one, and Jim, you hold the other, and I want you to stand over here next to the table. Closer together—a little closer . . . there." *Click, click, click.*

About two weeks later the tiny outfits began to arrive in the mail. Both sets of grandparents, all the aunts and uncles and great-aunts and great-uncles, all the cousins and cousins-in-law—*everyone* wanted to join up and march along in the baby twins parade.

Little sailor suits arrived. Then came the little Superman pajamas. Then little cowboy outfits, little baseball uniforms, little train conductor hats and overalls and vests, along with tiny sneakers and slippers and sandals and cowboy boots. And everything matched, just like the boys.

Everyone who sent something said, "Now, you be sure to send me a picture of how the twins look wearing these things, all right? And be sure to write on the back of the picture which boy is which, because *I* sure can't tell!"

And when the twins were dressed alike with their hair combed alike, little Jay and little Ray were cute. They were. They were unbelievably cute. Unbearably cute. Dangerously cute. Cute, cute, cute. And spot-on identical.

And if Mom or Dad took them out for a walk in their new superlong double stroller, someone would always stop, and bend down, and then say, "Oooh, look! There are *two* of them. Aren't they *cute*?"

And the answer to that always had to be yes. Yes, they were cute. Unfailingly, remarkably, and undeniably cute. So cute you could just eat 'em up. So cute you had to pat each of them on the head or tickle them under their adorable little chinny-chin-chins. So cute you just *had* to have a picture of them.

At naptime and at bedtime and at bath time, and even during a meal sometimes, Mom and Dad had to do the freckle-check. Because the boy with the

tiny freckle on his right ankle, that was Ray. *Right ankle, Ray. Right ankle, Ray—don't forget that. Right ankle, Ray.*

Because it was important to keep calling Ray by the name of Ray, and to keep calling Jay by the name of Jay. Wouldn't want the boys to get confused about their names, right? Because somewhere in the back of their minds, Jim and Sue Grayson actually did understand that these boys of theirs were two different people. Or that they would eventually *become* two different people . . . one day. Like, when they grew up . . . right?

When the boys got to be toddlers, Sue Grayson kept on dressing them alike. It made shopping for clothes a lot easier—in fact, it made clothes shopping twice as easy: two of this, two of that, two of these, two of those—all done.

And it also made getting the boys dressed a lot simpler—in fact, it made getting them dressed twice as simple: two of this, two of that, two of these, two of those—all matched up, all dressed. No muss, no fuss. And as the boys got a little older, dressing them the same also meant no arguments about which boy got to wear which shirts or pants or socks or shoes.

Then came school.

The twins became instant kindergarten celebrities. Everyone thought they were special. And cute. Very, very cute. And their teachers also thought they were adorable. And precious. And sweet. And dear. And darling. And charming.

The boys were a little small for their age, with straight brown hair and bright brown eyes, and shy smiles that made their right cheeks dimple in exactly the same places. And of course, no one could ever tell which twin was which.

Almost right away other kids started calling the boys names like "Ray-or-Jay" and "Jay-or-Ray." Some kids always used the name Ray, and some always used Jay, and then just paused—in case the twin needed to say, "No, I'm Jay," or "No, I'm Ray."

And some kids wouldn't even guess. They'd just say, "Hey, you." Or "Hi . . . guys."

The Grayson twins got tired of always having to correct people about their names. And they got tired of always seeing that question mark in the eyes of the kids at school, and even their teachers—a puzzled look that meant, *Now . . . which one are you?* That's why Ray and Jay stopped dressing alike shortly after they started second grade.

And to help everyone out a little, Ray almost

always wore a shirt or a sweater or a T-shirt or a baseball cap that had some red in it—red for Ray. And Jay usually wore something that was blue— blue for Jay, like the blue jay. And for the kids who actually cared about knowing which boy went with which name, the color-coded clothing helped. A little.

But the truth is, not that many kids tried to become really good friends with Jay and Ray. Because, like, how do you make two new friends at once? And if you wanted to get to know just one of the twins, which one would you pick? And if you did get to be friends with one of them, would that make the other twin feel left out?

Some kids also felt that most of the time Jay and Ray didn't really look like they even needed another friend. Because those two? They always had each other. It was like Ray and Jay got to have a sleepover with their best friend every single night of the week.

And that was true . . . sort of. Ray and Jay were certainly best friends. But it wasn't like they had gotten to choose that best friend. From the first moment of their lives, that other person who looked and talked and smiled exactly the same way was always there—eating at the same table, sleeping in the same room, riding on the same school bus, sitting in the same classroom. And almost no one was able to see any difference at all. Except Jay and Ray themselves.

During fifth grade the mix-ups had gotten worse. Like the time in February when Ray had been walking along the street near their home in Colorado, and this eighth-grade guy came charging up, shoved him into a slushy puddle, grabbed his book bag, emptied it onto the ground, and then shouted, "*That's* for hitting me in the face with that snowball last week!" Which seemed like a fair payback. Except it was Jay who had thrown the snowball, not Ray.

Or like the time last April when a girl had slipped a note into Jay's hand as he walked down the hallway at school, and it had taken the poor guy three days to figure out that the girl had a crush on Ray, not on him.

And the worst had been during the last half of fifth grade, when Jay had decided to go all out and earn the top grade in math. He'd done all his homework, studied hard for every test, even turned in the weekly extra-credit assignments. And on his final report card, Jay got a C− in math—and Ray got an A+. The math teacher had gotten their names and grades completely confused. The mistake eventually got fixed, but Jay felt cheated out of his moment of triumph, and Ray felt like he'd been shown up by his brainy brother. Again.

By the time they turned twelve years old in August, Ray and Jay were fed up with always being "the twins." They hated how they were constantly compared with each other. And there was no way to escape it.

At their last school, if you had asked a classmate, "What's Jay like?" you'd have probably gotten a shrug. Or maybe someone would have said, "Jay? He's . . . he's just like Ray."

And if you had asked someone, "Is Ray your friend?" you might have gotten another shrug. Or maybe someone would have said, "Sure—I mean, I guess he's my friend. Because I'm kind of friends with both of them. They're both nice. Except . . . I really can't tell which one is which. Unless one of them stays home sick or something."

And *that* was exactly what had happened to Jay Grayson on his first day of sixth grade in Clifton, Ohio. His twin brother Ray had stayed home sick.

Which was a good thing. Sort of. Maybe.

CHAPTER 3

TWINLESS

Duzing homeroom on his first day of sixth grade, Jay didn't ask Mrs. Lane why she hadn't called Ray's name. He thought, *Mom probably called the office and told them Ray was going to be absent, except . . . how come the desk right behind me isn't empty?* But there were a million other things to think about, so Jay just went along with the flow.

Mrs. Lane handed out everyone's class schedules, and Jay instantly had plenty of other things on his mind—like, how was he going to find his way around the new school? Language arts would be easy, because he'd be right back here with Mrs. Lane for eighth period. Everything else was a mystery.

But Alex said, "Almost all our classrooms are right here in the sixth-grade hall. And we have almost the same schedule."

So that was a help, and when the bell for first

period rang, Jay just followed Alex down the hall to the math room.

"Mrs. Pell," Alex said over his shoulder. "She's supposed to be really hard."

Then, as the class began and the teacher called the roll, the same thing happened.

"Jay Grayson?"

"Present."

"Alex Grellman?"

"Present."

No Ray Grayson.

And Jay thought the same thing: *All the teachers must know that Ray's absent today.*

So when Ray's name wasn't called during art or social studies, Jay hardly noticed.

But an hour or two later, when he opened his lunch bag, he found a note from his mom, and it was taped onto a second note. His mom had written:

Jay, please give this to the secretary in the school office.

And the second note said:

Jay's twin brother Ray is home today with a fever.

Mrs. Susan Grayson

Then after lunch, during seventh period, when all the sixth-grade boys had gym class together, Jay took a quick look at the attendance list on Mr. Bolton's clipboard. It showed the name of every sixth-grade boy in alphabetical order. And . . . no Ray Grayson.

And that's when Jay thought, *What's going on?*

But on that first Tuesday, Jay didn't ask any of his teachers about it. He didn't say, *Hey, I've got a twin brother, you know.* And Jay sort of forgot to give his mom's note to the school secretary—accidentally on purpose.

Because Jay knew that Ray would probably come to school on Wednesday, and then there would be the usual big deal about how the two of them looked *exactly* alike. And the comparing would begin. And there would be the usual staring and pointing, the usual oohing and aahing, the usual whispering and nodding.

And the usual teasing, too. Because at every other school they had ever attended, there always seemed to be some big, tough-looking kid who would say something like, "Aw, wook at da wittle twinsies—awen't dey *cute?*"

So Jay decided to keep himself totally unconnected from his twin brother, just for today.

Because being on his own was a nice change—very nice. He looked like no one else, he talked like no one else, he walked like no one else, he smiled like no one else. For this one day, Jay Grayson was twinless, purely himself. He was a regular, one-of-a-kind kid. And all day long, it felt great.

When Jay walked home after the first day of school, he let himself in at the kitchen door, walked into the living room, and flopped into a chair.

Mrs. Grayson had stayed home from work to take care of Ray, and she called from the upstairs room where she and her husband had set up a small office. "Is that you, Jay?"

"Yup," he called back. "It's me."

"Welcome home, sweetheart. How was your first day of school?"

And Jay called, "Good. It was good."

"I've just got to finish up a few e-mails, and then I'll come down and get you a snack. And I want you to tell me all about your day, all right?"

And Jay answered, "Okay."

His twin brother Ray was on the couch in front of the TV, picking a tune on his little nylon-stringed guitar. He stopped playing, looked over at Jay, raised one eyebrow, and said, "So?"

And Jay said, "So, what?"

"So how was it really?"

Jay shrugged. "It was good. Really."

"Good in what way?" Ray said. "How about the teachers? What are they like?" And he plucked a few more notes on his guitar.

It kind of bugged Jay that Ray had gotten so good at playing the guitar—he'd only had it for about six months. And Ray was a good singer, too.

Jay said, "What are the teachers like? Do you mean, are any of them professional wrestlers? No. And none of them are NASCAR drivers, either. Or movie stars. They're *teachers*, Ray. Just teachers. A bunch of women, a couple guys—teachers. They teach stuff. To kids. And I said school was good because everything was pretty much like school should be. Pretty much like all our other schools have been for the past six years."

Ignoring the sarcasm, Ray said, "How about girls?"

Jay nodded, staring at the TV. "Yes, there were girls at school today."

"Any cute ones?" Ray asked, with another run of notes on the guitar.

Jay said, "Look, Ray, you're gonna see the whole setup for yourself tomorrow, okay? And you can decide for yourself if the girls are cute or not, and if the teachers are okay, and if the cafeteria food stinks. Some of us went to school today and worked, and some of us would just like to sit and watch TV for a while. Without answering a million questions."

"Fine," Ray said. "Just pretend I never asked."

"I will," Jay said.

And Ray said, "Fine—go ahead and keep the whole stupid day all to yourself."

"I will," Jay said.

And Ray said, "Fine."

And Jay said, "Good. Now how about you shut up for a while? And don't play the guitar, either."

And Jay pretended to give his full attention to the old TV Western that Ray had been watching. Except Jay felt guilty, shutting Ray out like that.

Because to tell the truth, Ray had picked up on how his brother was feeling. Jay really did want to keep the whole day for himself. He didn't want to share what had happened at school, because this first day had been *his*, all his.

And there was another reason Jay didn't want to talk about it. He didn't want to be forced to admit that he had loved being on his own all day.

Because he had. He had really enjoyed being at school *without* being a twin. A lot. And he didn't want to tell that to Ray. It seemed disloyal. Almost mean.

So Jay kept it to himself.

But to tell the *whole* truth, Ray had also enjoyed being twinless all day. It had been a long car trip from Colorado to Ohio, trapped in Labor Day weekend traffic in the back of the minivan. With Jay. So even though he wasn't feeling great, Tuesday had been a welcome break for Ray. For almost eight hours straight he had gotten to choose exactly what he wanted to do—without any discussion, without one sarcastic comment, without the constant observation of that other pair of eyes. When Ray had watched TV, there had been no arguments about the programs, no wrestling for the remote. And there had been no complaints about his guitar playing. Plus, at lunch, Ray had gotten to eat all six of the last Oreos in the house—no dividing things up evenly. It had been a great day.

Ray was feeling a lot better by dinnertime on Tuesday, but he pretended to be sicker than he was. He didn't want to have to get up the next morning and face the new school—plus deal with being "one of those new twins." So he coughed a lot more than he needed to. And he picked at his food, then pushed his plate away. And instead of digging into a bowl of chocolate ice cream, Ray said, "I want to go lie down."

And it worked: On Wednesday, Ray got to stay home again, and he was glad.

And on Wednesday, Jay walked the three blocks to school by himself. Again. And he was glad too.

CHAPTER 4

TWICE AS THICK

Jay arrived a little early for his second day of school, so he walked around back to the playground. It was crowded, but right away he spotted Alex's bright blond hair. He walked over and said, "Hey, Alex—yesterday I forgot to ask where your hockey team practices."

Alex told him all about Clifton's new municipal rink, which was only about a mile from his house. "Yeah, it's great ice, and all the leagues raised money, and we just got a new Zamboni." Then Alex said, "You play hockey?"

Jay shook his head. "Nah, just pond hockey sometimes." And Jay almost said, *But my twin brother, Ray? He's really good. He should definitely be on a team.* And it was true. Skating was the one sport where Ray was a lot better than he was. But Jay didn't say that. He didn't want to get into any talk about his brother. So he changed the subject and asked Alex what his favorite books were. That conversation didn't go very far, and the two of them ended up talking about *The Simpsons* until the first bell rang and everyone lined up to go inside.

Once again, Mrs. Lane didn't call Ray's name during attendance in homeroom. And once again, Jay noticed, but he didn't think much about it— until a few minutes later when he read the label on a cardboard file box sitting on a chair beside the teacher's desk: 6-A STUDENT FOLDERS. That made Jay curious, because it still seemed odd that no one was calling Ray's name in any of his classes. But homeroom ended, and he rushed off to his first class.

Jay liked math, and he liked his new teacher, too. She was one of those no-nonsense people who hated to waste time. Mrs. Pell opened the class with a quick review of the readiness test they had taken on Tuesday, and then she had their new math books passed out in about two minutes. She said, "We're going to jump right into factoring. It's important because it's going to make working with equations and expressions a lot easier for you . . . a *lot*. So no complaining, okay? Now, flip to page seventy-two in your books. Anybody think they remember this stuff well enough to factor all the numbers in problem number one?"

Jay shot his hand into the air, but so did five or six other kids, and he wasn't called on. But the fifth problem was about finding prime factors— and his was the only hand that went up. And standing at the board, he used a method that he had learned in fifth grade.

Mrs. Pell nodded and said, "Can someone else explain what Jay did here?"

By this time Jay was back at his desk. A girl raised her hand. He turned to look at her.

When the teacher nodded, the girl said, "It's sort of like he used upside-down division. In a big stack."

The teacher nodded again. "That's right, Rachel, and he divided every number until only prime numbers were left. And Jay, what's the definition of a prime number?"

After a pause, the teacher said, "The definition? Jay?"

Jay was still looking at Rachel, the girl in the first row by the windows.

He snapped his head toward Mrs. Pell and said, "A prime number can only be divided by itself and the number one."

Jay's face felt hot, because he was sure everyone had seen him staring. At that girl. But the lesson moved ahead briskly, and no one had time to think about anything but the next problems. Even so, Jay managed to sneak a few more looks over toward the windows.

After math class, Jay started talking with a tall, sandy-haired kid named James. And a couple of periods later during lunch, James called to him across the cafeteria and motioned for Jay to come sit with him and some of his other friends. Then they all hung out on the playground during after-lunch recess and started up a game of basketball against some other guys.

Jay was the smallest boy on the basketball court, but he was quick on his feet, and he had good ball-handling skills. Twice in a row he fed James with a perfect inside pass, and each time the taller boy scored. And as Jay played, going all out to impress these new kids, he was suddenly very aware that Ray wasn't around.

Jay knew that in most sports, Ray wasn't quite as good an athlete as he was. And whenever they played on the same team, everyone else knew it too. That's what it had been like playing Little League baseball together in Colorado. Jay had been a star outfielder and the number three hitter on the team, and Ray . . . hadn't. Jay never held back, but he always felt bad for his brother. Because he knew that everyone automatically compared them to each other. And today, right now? It was nice not to have to think about that.

When the bell rang and the guys walked back inside together, someone started talking about the Winter Olympics, and Jay jumped in and started telling James about a huge blizzard that had hit Denver last winter.

And Jay almost said, *Yeah, my brother Ray and I? We built this* amazing *snow fort in our backyard!* But he didn't. He didn't want to get into stuff about family. And brothers. And being a twin. Not with James, not with anyone.

Because it was only the second day of school, and already Jay felt like he was beginning to make some friends. On his own. And so far, no one had needed to ask, "Which one are you—Jay or Ray?"

Still, it seemed strange that not one teacher had even mentioned Ray's name yet. Jay thought, *It's like a Hardy Boys mystery or something*—The Case of the Missing Twin.

So during language arts class on the afternoon

of that second day, Jay did a little snooping. Because that file box of student folders he had noticed in the morning during homeroom was still sitting on a chair beside Mrs. Lane's desk.

Even though he didn't need help with the grammar review sheet the class was working on, Jay pretended he did—so that he could stand in the line at the teacher's desk. And as he stood there, he took a careful look and saw his own folder. The folder was bright blue, the only blue one in the box. His name was printed on a label, plain as day: Grayson, Jay Ray.

And the folder for Grayson, Ray Jay? Not there. Missing.

And then Jay noticed something else. *His* folder looked way too thick. In fact, that bright blue student folder looked more than *twice* as thick as any of the other ones.

And in a flash, Jay understood exactly why none of the teachers had been calling his brother's name during attendance.

And in a second flash, Jay knew exactly what to do about that.

CHAPTER 5

DEAL

"You're crazy!"

That's what Ray said to Jay on Wednesday afternoon.

Because when Jay came home from his second day at school, he told his twin brother what had happened to their school record folders—how two sets of information had been stuffed into one folder, *his* folder.

"So it's like the school completely lost your records!" Jay said, his eyes wide and wild. He was having a hard time keeping his voice low so their father wouldn't hear from the upstairs office. It had been Dad's turn to work from home today and take care of Ray.

Jay said, "They think there's only *one* of us. So only one of us has to go to school, and I've got it all planned out—it's gonna be great! We *have* to do this, Ray, we *have* to! Don't you *see*?"

Ray snorted. "All I see is some kid who's completely insane. I mean, sure, it might be fun and everything, but you *know* we'd get caught. Then what?"

Jay said, "Then . . . then we'll go to the principal's office. And we'll probably get yelled at, and Mom and Dad will be mad for a few days, and maybe we'll get grounded for a couple weeks. But so what? Remember that time in third grade when Kenny March started shoving you around on the playground, and we both tackled him? And we got sent to the principal's office? No big deal, right?"

Ray shook his head. "That was self-defense. That kid was a bully, and everybody knew it. This? This'll be like . . . like telling a million lies. Every time someone looks at me and says, 'Hi, Jay' and I say, 'Hi'—that's a lie. And every time Mom says 'How was school today?' and you weren't there, and you say, 'Fine'—that'll be another lie. It'll go on and on, and then we'll get caught, and someone's gonna get up in your face and say, 'Why in the world did you want to *do* something like this?'"

Jay said, "And then I'll say, 'We did this because . . . it was an experiment. Because we *had* to find out how it would feel to be one person, instead of always being part of a pair, and always having everyone stare and point at us.'" Jay paused. "Besides, we're not the ones who lost that folder. That was the school's fault, right?"

Ray rolled his eyes. "That is so lame—blaming it on the school. And then you're gonna say, 'Boo-hoo, I'm a poor little twin and no one understands me?' Lame."

"Oh," Jay said, "so when no one ever really knows if you're you, or if you're me, you *like* that, right?"

"No," said Ray, "but—"

Jay interrupted, "I mean, think of it, Ray—*every other day* you could stay home! And do whatever you wanted to. And when you *do* go to school, you'll be completely on your own there. You've *got* to try it out, Ray. No offense or anything, but *not* being a twin? At school? It's really great."

Ray made a face. "Except everyone at school would think that I'm *you*."

"Well," Jay said, "yeah . . . but it's sort of like *you* would be invisible or something. Like, if you do something really stupid, who gets the blame? Jay Grayson. It's like you've got a free pass."

"Don't be an idiot," said Ray. "I'd still look like a jerk, because if we get caught—I mean *when* we get caught—I'm gonna look twice as dumb for going along with this in the first place. I'll be the kid who was pretending to be his crazy twin brother."

"No," Jay said, "you'll be the kid who's famous for being almost as good-looking and almost as smart and clever and talented as his fabulous twin brother."

"Ha, ha, very funny," Ray said. "Can we stop talking about this now?"

Jay leaned closer and narrowed his eyes. "So . . . Ray Grayson is saying that he has never wished that his twin brother would disappear for a week or two, never wished he could see what it was like to be all on his own?" Jay paused. "And Ray Grayson has never wished he could meet some new kids and just be . . . himself?"

The twins looked at each other for a long moment. It was like looking into a mirror. And Jay could see Ray thinking. And Jay knew what Ray was going to say before he said it.

"All right," Ray said. "I'm in." He raised his eyebrows, "*But* . . . I'm only trying it out for one day, okay?"

Jay raised his eyebrows too and nodded. "Whenever you want to stop, we stop."

Ray said, "And also, *you* have to pretend to be *me* staying home sick tomorrow . . ."

". . . which would keep us *both* out of trouble," Jay finished, "in case there was a problem at school. Brilliant! Except no way is there gonna be a problem. I'm telling you, nobody at school has any idea that Ray Grayson even exists." Jay stuck out his right hand. "So . . . we've got a deal, right?"

Ray nodded. "Deal."

And the Grayson brothers shook on it.

CHAPTER 6

THROUGH THE MIRROR

It was Thursday morning, the third day of school, and right after the Pledge of Allegiance Mrs. Lane took attendance, just like always. And after calling out more than a dozen names, she said, "Jay Grayson?"

And he answered, "Present."

But the boy who said that wasn't Jay. It was Ray.

Ray had had no trouble finding his locker, dialing the combination, getting his books, finding his homeroom. He had a good map worked out inside his head, so everything was right where he expected it to be. Taft Elementary School looked exactly the way Jay had described it.

Ray felt perfectly at ease striking up a conversation about hockey with Alex during homeroom. He felt zero awkwardness, zero shyness, zero anxiety—about anything. New school, new town? No sweat. Ray decided that Jay had done a fantastic job dealing with the first few days—like a stuntman who does all the dangerous stuff so the movie star can step into the scene and have some fun.

And after homeroom, when a tall, sandy-haired kid smiled at him in the hall on the way to math and called out, "Hi, Jay," Ray smiled back and called out, "Hey, James." Because James looked just the way Jay had said he would.

But first-period math class brought some unexpected problems. The situation reminded Ray of their collection of Star Wars action figures. Because he and Jay used to pop off the heads and switch them around to make new characters. If you plug Boba Fett's head onto Luke's body, you've got Boba-Lu. Or Princess Leia's head on Chewbacca's body makes Chewleia. And right now, it was Jay's body with Ray's head on it. And in math class, that wasn't so good.

Ray really had to struggle to keep up as the teacher started going over the homework, and when they got to the sixth problem, Mrs. Pell looked right at him and said, "Jay, you did such a good job with that prime factoring problem yesterday that I left the problem on the board to show to the afternoon class. Come up front and work this one out for us."

Ray gulped, and smiled, and almost panicked. There was no way he could work that problem. So he had to use his wit and charm—something Jay would not have been able to pull off.

With just a trace of a smile on his face, Ray said, "Actually, I think that would be selfish of me. Someone else should get a turn today." Which got a big laugh from the kids in the class. And a small smile from the teacher. But Mrs. Pell nodded and said, "That sounds fair," and she called on someone else.

Ray managed to survive to the end of math class. And he even got used to everyone calling him by his brother's name. After all, ever since he was born, almost everyone he'd ever met had been calling him Jay now and then . . . including his own mom and dad.

And after walking through the hallways, meeting new kids, and talking to teachers, Ray found himself sitting in art class during third period, sketching a vase of dried flowers. And glancing around the sunlit room, it hit him: Not one single kid, *no one* in the whole school, had any idea at all that he was an identical twin. At this moment he was just one person, unique.

And for the first time he could remember, Ray

got a glimpse of himself that way—as a single person, completely unconnected to any other. It was a shocker. Because for twelve years, whenever Ray had been out in public, Jay had usually been there too. So Ray had thought of himself as a twin. And he had always expected everyone else to see him that way too—as part of a pair, as a fraction: one-half of The Grayson Brothers Amazing Traveling Twin Show.

Ray decided that Jay had told him the truth: *Not being a twin at school was a great experience.* And so far, it was absolutely worth the risk.

But there was no risk, not today. Or none that Ray could see. The box of folders that Jay had described, the box next to Mrs. Lane's desk that contained that extra-thick blue file? On Thursday morning the box was gone. Ray was pretty sure that the folders were back in the office now, stuck away in a closet or a cabinet somewhere, filed away for the rest of the year. And Ray Grayson . . . wasn't. Just *wasn't*.

Ray didn't really like that. To be wiped out, to be missing—his name just blotted out? Yes, it was making this amazing day possible, and he was definitely having a blast, but Ray had mixed feelings about it . . . that is, until science class right after lunch.

Because this was the day that Mrs. Abbot assigned lab partners. And Jay Grayson was paired up with Melissa Rollins. Which meant that Ray found himself sitting next to the prettiest girl he had ever seen.

And she smiled at him.

It was a dazzling smile, and Melissa didn't try to hide that she thought Ray was . . . interesting. And he wasn't interesting because he had an identical twin brother. He was interesting all on his own. Him . . . Ray. Interesting.

Except . . . this girl thought his name was Jay. Like everyone else.

But suddenly, what Melissa thought his name might be wasn't so important. What mattered was that smile of hers. And that she had beamed that smile at *him*—Ray Grayson. Because no matter what she thought his name was, the boy sitting next to her was definitely Ray. Definitely.

When the teacher was busy up at the front of the room, Melissa leaned toward him and whispered, "So you're new here in Clifton, right?" Another smile.

Ray nodded. "Just moved to town four days ago."

"Do you like it here?" she asked.

He smiled and nodded. "More and more."

And Ray wasn't kidding.

And by the end of science class, Ray felt like Melissa Rollins just might become an important part of his sixth-grade year.

At home, Jay was on the phone with his mom. It was the third time she had called to check on him, because both parents had gone to the office today.

"I'm feeling good, Mom. Really. I'm sure I'll be able to go to school tomorrow."

"That's good, sweetheart. Well, we'll be home about five, okay? And will you go to the freezer when we're off the phone and take out a pound of ground beef? We're having spaghetti tonight."

"Sure, Mom, no problem."

"Now listen, Ray, I don't want you to fall behind in your work. So when Jay gets home, be sure to get your homework assignments and get started on them right away, all right?"

Jay said, "I will."

"Good. See you later, Ray. I love you."

"Love you too, Mom. Bye."

And as he hung up, Jay tried to count how many times he had lied to his mom so far today. He lost track somewhere between fifteen and twenty.

CHAPTER 7

MESSY

At 3:27 on Thursday afternoon, even before Ray had his key out of the lock on the kitchen door, Jay was right there, blasting him with questions.

"So what do you think? Was I right? Did you have a good day? Meet any new kids? It was great, right? It's a nice school, don't you think?"

Ray smiled. "It was just like you said. Almost feels like I've never been to school before—it's a whole new thing."

"Did you like James?" Jay asked. "He's a great guy. Did you hang out with him at lunch?"

Ray nodded. "Yeah, I like him. And that other kid, the one with the red hair?"

"Sean, right?" Jay said.

"Yeah, Sean. He's a good kid too, really funny at lunch," Ray said. He looked around at the mess on the kitchen counters. "So what did you do all day?"

Jay smiled. "Watched a couple TV shows, took a nap, downloaded this new skateboarding game, ate lunch, played the game until my thumbs started hurting, finished one book and started another one, had some snacks, took another nap. Great day."

Ray frowned. "What about the social studies report on ancient cultures that's due next Wednesday? Did you do any of the reading for that? Because in class today it sounded like Mr. Fulton is a tough grader."

Jay shrugged. "Relax—there's plenty of time. Besides, I'm sick today, remember? So what else happened at school?"

"Nothing much," Ray said, "except . . . I met this girl. In science this afternoon."

Jay pretended to be amazed, but he wasn't. Ray was always meeting girls. "You don't say. A girl. His first day at the new school, and Ray meets a girl. So . . . you sort of like this girl?"

Ray grinned. "Yeah, sort of."

"Interesting," Jay said. "So what's her name?"

"Melissa, and she's my lab partner. And I think she sort of likes me, too."

Jay said, "You mean, she sort of likes *us*, right?"

Ray's smile vanished. "No, she likes me. *Me.*"

"Right," Jay said. "She likes her new lab partner . . . Jay Grayson."

It took Ray about three seconds to wrestle Jay to the ground and pin his face against the cold tile of the kitchen floor.

"She likes *me*, you got it? *Me.*" Ray was talking through clenched teeth. "And you're not going to mess this up, right?"

"Okay, okay," Jay said. "I promise I won't let her see me picking our nose."

Ray twisted Jay's arm. "Not funny, Jay."

Jay swung his legs around, shifted his weight, pushed up with his free arm, and three seconds later it was Ray's nose pressed against the floor. Because whenever things got physical, the twins were a dead-even match for each other.

Panting a little from the effort, Jay said, "If this girl thinks *you're* cute, she's gonna go nuts about me. So don't worry. We'll be a good team. Just let me know when you two start kissing, okay? I want to be ready for that."

Ray struggled but couldn't break free. "I'm gonna kill you, Jay."

Jay said, "Maybe someday, but not today. Listen, though—I'm just kidding, okay? I'm kidding.

I'll be nice to this Melissa girl. *Your* Melissa. Truce, okay? Truce."

Ray nodded and said, "Truce."

The boys peeled themselves apart and then sat there on the kitchen floor, back to back, breathing hard.

After a minute Ray said, "Y' know what? I think one day was enough for me. I mean, maybe I could pretend to be sick one more day, and you could go to school on Friday by yourself again. If you want to. But on Monday, we should both go to school. Let the office people discover that they've got a lost kid. Because right now, I stayed home sick, and you didn't give Mom's note to the office. That's all that's happened so far. And on Monday I show up at school, and my missing file gets found, and that'll be the end of it. Okay with you?"

"So . . .," Jay said, "on Monday we start the school year all over again. As twins. 'Hi, everybody, guess what? We're the twins, Ray and Jay.' That's what you want to do. On Monday, right?"

Ray didn't answer immediately, so Jay went on, choosing his words carefully. "Because if it was all up to me? I'd keep going a while with this. Just because it's so . . . interesting. I mean, it's fun and everything too. But mostly it's just so . . . new.

Being out there by myself a little. I mean, after high school, if we go to different colleges or something? Then we'll be on our own, really on our own. But that's a long time away. And this? This is right *now*. Like, didn't you think today was really fun?"

Ray said, "Of course it was fun. And I liked the whole other thing too, being on my own. But it's gonna fall apart—it *has* to. And then, *boom*, big trouble. Big. Like, *really* big trouble."

"Maybe not so big," Jay said. "More like medium. Medium trouble. And for something like this? I think that might be worth it."

They were still sitting on the floor, back to back, like a pair of bookends.

"I don't know," Ray said. "It's just so . . . messy. Like, with the assignments and the friends and everything."

Jay said, "You mean, like with that girl, right?"

And Ray could hear the smile in Jay's voice, so he elbowed his brother in the back.

"Not just that," Ray said. "I mean . . . everything. It's all messy."

"How about this," Jay said. "How about we keep it going for another week, just until next Friday. Then we'll confess, we'll say we're very sorry, we'll explain whatever we need to, and then we'll go back to being the twins. But let's just see what happens, okay? For another week. To next Friday."

Ray said, "You're insane—you know that, right? My twin brother is officially crazy. *Scary* crazy."

A long pause, and Jay said nothing.

Then Ray started to laugh. "And me? I'm even scarier. Because I *know* how crazy you are, and I keep going along with you. Which makes me worse, much worse. Meet Ray and Jay, the craziest twins on Earth. And next Friday? That's when we become the saddest, most punished twins in human history."

"Maybe," Jay said. He stood up, then reached down and pulled Ray to his feet. He kept hold of his brother's hand, and with a big grin he said, "But I'll tell you what. This is going to be a *great* week, a week to remember—maybe the greatest week ever."

"And the messiest," said Ray. "So . . . is there any food left around here, or did you eat it all? Because I need some serious snack action."

"There's a ton of food," Jay said, "and you're gonna need it too. For the energy. Because the last time Mom talked to you—I mean, when she talked to me when I was pretending to be you—she said that when I got home from school today, you had to get all the assignments so you could be caught up when you go back to school tomorrow. Because you told her that you were feeling a lot better today. I mean, *I* told her you were feeling better. So, do you have a lot of homework for tomorrow?"

"Me?" Ray said. "No, but *you've* got homework. Tons. Because this is the way it has to work, otherwise I'm out: The guy who goes to school does the homework that's due on the day he goes. And tomorrow is *my* day off. But I took really good notes today—much better than the ones you took yesterday. That factoring stuff in math? Almost killed me. And *you've* got to do a better job of writing down the assignments. So that I can do a good job on *your* homework . . . which *I* will have to turn in when I go to school and pretend to be you. On Monday."

Jay said, "Let's just eat something, okay? We'll get all the details worked out. 'Cause two heads are better than one, right?"

As Ray opened the refrigerator, he looked over his shoulder at Jay and said, "I'm not so sure about that anymore."

CHAPTER 8

HOME BOY

An hour before homeroom on Friday, Ray and Jay got up, showered, got dressed, made their beds, ate breakfast, picked up their lunches, grabbed their book bags, kissed their mom and dad good-bye, and headed off for school.

Except Ray took a detour.

Just outside the kitchen door, he ducked below the level of the windows, scooted between the bushes, scurried around the corner, went behind the house, opened the back door to the garage, and slipped inside.

Before their parents had come home from work on Thursday afternoon, Jay and Ray had spent some time in the garage. It was a one-car garage, and it was almost filled with tall stacks of cardboard boxes that hadn't been unpacked yet. The brothers had hollowed out a six-foot square of hidden floor space by rearranging the mess and then piling boxes up and around. It was sort of like building an igloo. And inside this cardboard igloo they had put a folding lawn chair, a flashlight, a few comic books, an iPod Ray had loaded with some songs he wanted to learn, and five or six of Jay's favorite paperbacks.

So after making his way to the garage Friday morning, Ray got onto his hands and knees, pushed one box aside, stuffed his book bag ahead of him, and wriggled into the hideout. Then he pulled the box back to cover the opening, felt around in the dark until he found the lawn chair, carefully got to his feet, and sat down.

And then he waited, flashlight off, barely daring to breathe, just listening to the heartbeats pounding away in his chest.

Ten minutes later, which felt more like ten hours, Ray heard his mom and dad walk outside and pull the kitchen door shut behind them. He heard two car doors open and then slam, heard their old minivan start up and drive away.

Ray crawled from his hiding place, pushed the box back to cover the opening, and peeked to be sure the coast was clear. Then he opened the side door of the garage, took two quick steps across the

narrow breezeway to the kitchen door, opened it with his key, and went inside.

Soon Ray was sprawled on the living-room couch enjoying a second bowl of cereal. And when he flipped on the TV, he discovered some great old detective movies that were just starting up on a classic film channel—four movies in a row. And fifteen minutes into the first movie, he was sound asleep, slumped sideways on the couch with his head on a pillow, his guitar within easy reach.

Ray woke up an hour or so later, just as a scar-faced man wearing a wide-brimmed hat began firing a huge machine gun into the side of a speeding car. Ray yawned, stretched, smiled, and closed his eyes again. He thought, *Yes indeed, life is sweet. I could get used to this.*

And for the second day in a row, Ray had a feeling he hadn't known for a long time. He felt like being a twin was wonderful.

But as he began to doze off, he couldn't help wondering what was happening at school. Sure, it was nice to kick back at home, but school was definitely where the action was. Definitely.

CHAPTER 9

ASSIGNMENTS

Jay didn't know what to do. He was sitting in Friday's first-period math class, and this girl had just smiled his way. It wasn't Rachel, the girl who had talked about his factoring problem on Wednesday. This was a different girl, even cuter, and she had smiled right at him.

He wanted to smile back. *That's gotta be Melissa, the girl Ray met yesterday,* he thought. *So it's okay if I smile at her, right? But . . . what if that's not her?*

He gulped, then looked past her and stared at the bulletin board, pretending he hadn't seen her.

Jay wished he had paid better attention to everyone's name when Mrs. Pell was taking attendance. And he wished he had gotten a more detailed description of Melissa from Ray. *Because if I smile back, and this is some other cute girl, then that could mess things up for Ray. And if it is Melissa, and I smile at her, and then she comes over and starts talking to me after class, then . . . like, what do I say to her?*

Talking to girls was not Jay's best skill. When it came to girls, he was a little in awe of his twin brother—not that he would have ever told Ray that. But it was true. Ray always knew just what to say to girls, how to flirt and joke around, how to keep a conversation light and funny. And the girls seemed to like that. In Colorado, Ray had even sort of had a girlfriend for the last month of fifth grade.

Jay was just as interested in girls as Ray was— maybe even more. But Jay liked to admire girls from a comfortable distance. When he got to science class after lunch? Then he'd solve the mystery of Melissa's identity. And maybe by then he could figure out what he should say to her.

So for the rest of math class, Jay kept his eyes on his book. And on his worksheet. And on the screen above the overhead projector, where Mrs. Pell was reviewing the order of algebraic operations.

And actually, Jay really needed to pay careful attention so he'd be able to explain all this stuff to Ray. Because Ray got along with girls a lot better than he got along with math.

Near the end of the class, when Jay wrote down

the math assignment for Monday, on the same page
he wrote:

> Tell Ray to check out the girl in
> math who sits in the second desk
> from the front in the row next to
> the windows. To see if she's
> Melissa.

But then he crossed that out, because he
thought, *That's stupid—I'll know if this girl is Melissa
the minute I get to science class.*
And instead he wrote:

> Tell Ray that if the girl in math
> class who sits in the second desk
> from the front in the third row
> from the windows isn't Melissa, he
> still has to be kind of nice to her
> if she smiles at him.

But then Jay crossed all that out too, because he
knew Ray would just tease him about this girl, no
matter who she was.

As math class ended, Jay avoided all chance of connecting with the mystery girl by hurrying out of the room and walking to music class with James.

James seemed to know everyone, and everyone seemed to like him. And being friends with a popular kid like James was something new for Jay.

As they stood inside the music room doorway, waiting for the bell, James said, "Hey, did you play soccer when you lived in Colorado last year?"

Jay nodded. "Yeah, I played some soccer."

Which was true, especially the part about "some." Because the only soccer Jay had ever played was during gym classes.

James said, "'Cause there's a sixth-grade team here. I mean, it's more like a club than a team. Sean plays too. And Mr. Parnell, the music teacher? He's the coach. And he's good. You're really quick on your feet, so I bet you'd get a good position, might even play forward. You should come to the first practice."

Jay was flattered that James had noticed how fast he was, and even more flattered to be asked to join this team, or club, or whatever it was. A bunch of guys kicking a soccer ball around? Sounded like fun.

So Jay smiled and nodded and said, "Yeah, I'll come. That'll be great."

The bell rang, and as they took their seats, Jay opened his assignment notebook and wrote:

Tell Ray he has to pretend he likes soccer.

That afternoon, just before sixth period, Jay identified Melissa by standing inside the door of the science room and locating lab table number nine—third one from the windows, second row from the back. And the girl sitting at table nine was a surprise to Jay—actually, a double surprise.

First, this girl was *not* the one who had smiled at him at the start of math class. So that was nice to know. And second, he was surprised that this girl wasn't prettier. From the way Ray had talked, Jay had expected to be blinded and astonished by Melissa's beauty. And he wasn't. He thought, *She's sort of cute. I can see that. Definitely.*

But as Jay took his seat at lab table number nine, the girl who turned and gave him a warm smile didn't seem so special. Not at all.

Still, Jay smiled back at her because he knew Ray would want him to. And he said, "Hey . . . hi."

And Melissa said, "Hi. I really like your shirt."

"Oh," Jay said. "Um . . . thanks. I . . . I like yours, too. Yeah, very nice shirt." Jay nodded. And even though he knew he'd said enough, he felt like he had to keep talking. "Shirts are great," he said. "Especially blue ones. Like yours. Because . . . that's a blue shirt, right?" She nodded, and Jay said, "I thought it was blue . . . yeah. Blue shirts . . . they're really great. Yeah. Blue."

Melissa kept smiling, but her eyes clouded over and her head began to tilt, sort of the way a dog tilts its head at a bug that's crawling on the floor.

Jay had seen that tilted-head look before. From other girls he had tried to talk to.

Before Jay could say anything else about shirts, Mrs. Abbot came to the rescue. "All right, everyone, quiet down now. The worksheets for your first lab are there on your tables. I've filled in a lot of the steps for you, because this is mostly a review of the scientific process. The materials you and your partner will need are on the long tables at the back of the room. Partners may talk to each other, but this isn't a time for socializing. Please begin now, and be sure to save the last five minutes of the period for cleaning up."

Papers rustled, chairs slid on the floor, and kids began moving around the room. And despite what

Mrs. Abbot had just said, a low buzz of chatter filled the room.

But Jay was frozen, afraid to move, afraid to say another word to his lab partner.

Melissa took charge. She said, "Here, take this sheet and go get the things we need, okay?"

Jay nodded. "Yeah. Good idea." He scooted his chair back and rushed away to join the crowd of kids headed for the back of the room. And when he returned—and for the next thirty-five minutes— the only thing going on at lab table number nine was science. It was strictly school business.

When class ended, Jay was amazed by how quickly Melissa gathered up her things and left the room. Without a smile, without a good-bye.

And in his assignment book he wrote:

Tell Ray he has to convince Melissa that Jay is not a dork.

And he thought, *Monday's gonna be a busy day at school. For Ray.*

CHAPTER 10

FULL-TIME JOB

"Hey, it's Friday—first weekend in Ohio! How about we go grab some pizza and a movie at the mall, and maybe get some new gym shoes for you two. How's that sound?"

Their parents had just gotten home from work, and it was Jay and Ray's dad talking, and he was making an offer no sixth-grade guy could refuse. But before either boy answered, they flashed each other a quick look, and silent alarms went off inside their heads. Until this moment, it hadn't dawned on either of them that *not* being twins was going to be a round-the-clock job.

Because if you pretend not to have a twin brother at school, you have to pretend not to have a twin brother everywhere else—especially at the mall on a Friday night. Kids from school could show up anywhere. And so could teachers.

All this took only half a second, and that glance the brothers exchanged meant, *Do we dare?*

Ray made a *No way!* face at Jay.

But Jay said, "Sounds great, Dad. Be ready in a minute."

Ray followed Jay upstairs to their room, and the second he shut the door he slugged Jay on the arm.

"Hey!" Jay said. "What's that for?"

"For being an idiot, that's what. The mall could be loaded with kids from school."

Jay said, "Relax, okay? I've got it all figured out."

As Ray watched, Jay opened the bottom drawer of their big dresser and pulled out a red hooded sweatshirt.

"That's mine," Ray said. "Put it back."

Jay shook his head. "Just watch."

He took off the shirt he'd worn to school, pulled on the hoodie, then went to the closet and got a St. Louis Cardinals hat, also Ray's. He yanked it onto his head almost down to his ears. Then he grabbed Ray's fake Oakley sunglasses from his side of the dresser, slipped them on, and pulled up the hood of the sweatshirt.

"See?" Jay said. "We're gonna let Mom and Dad think that I'm you tonight, and you're gonna be me. At the mall. And if we see any kids, they'll just think I'm your friend, somebody they don't know. And with you being Jay, if we just happen to run into Melissa, I won't have to try to pretend to be you—pretending to be me. I know the Melissa thing is a long shot, but if she's there tonight, you're gonna need to make a really good impression."

"What's that mean?" Ray said, his eyes narrowing.

Jay hadn't told Ray about his time with Melissa during sixth period. "Well," he said, "I don't think the *real* Jay was as smooth today as the fake Jay would have been. During science." He hurried to add, "It's nothing huge or anything, but *you* should definitely be the next Jay who talks to Melissa. Definitely."

Ray stared at his brother. "And you think your little disguise is gonna trick Mom and Dad?"

Jay said, "I'm betting yes. Here, put on the shirt I wore to school today, and wear my Cubs hat. And if Mom or Dad can tell us apart, then I'll stay home and eat leftover spaghetti. *And* work on the social studies report. Except let *me* do the talking. Deal?"

Ray rolled his eyes, but he said, "Deal." And then he changed into Jay's shirt and pulled on the blue baseball cap.

When the boys came down the stairs into the

living room, Mrs. Grayson took one look at Jay and said, "Sunglasses? There won't be much sunshine at the mall, Ray."

And Jay said, "I just like the way they look, okay?"

And his mom said, "Suit yourself."

Mr. Grayson got up off the couch. "I don't know about everybody else, but I'm starved. Let's get going."

And the family headed out the kitchen door.

Ray and Jay got to the doorway at the same time, so Ray shoved Jay out of his way, and then just outside the door Jay pushed Ray into the bushes, and then Ray slammed Jay up against the side of the garage, and then Jay knocked the Cubs hat off Ray's head.

"Boys, stop it!" said Mrs. Grayson. She glared at the boy wearing the sunglasses. "Ray, you stop this tough-guy act right now, or you can just stay home, got it?"

Jay pointed at Ray and said, "Jay started it." And he realized that he might get *himself* grounded. For telling what Ray had done.

Their dad said, "Just get in the van, both of you." He slid the side door open and pointed toward the third seat. "Jay, back there. Ray, sit in the middle."

So Ray sat in the backseat, and Jay sat in the center seat. And as the minivan backed out of the driveway, Jay turned around, pulled the sunglasses down, winked at Ray, and gave him a big thumbs-up sign. Because their disguises were working great. So far.

CHAPTER 11

WEEKEND WARRIORS

D inner at the mall went fine—no kids from school were sighted anywhere near the pizza place. And the early show at the Cineplex? No problem—the place was filled with complete strangers.

It was after the movie, on the long walk back through the mall to the shoe store. That's when things got dangerous.

Ray, dressed as Jay, and Jay, dressed as Ray, were walking about fifty feet behind their parents so it would look like they were at the mall on their own. And from somewhere over near the food court, a voice yelled out, "Hey, Jay—wait up!"

Ray stopped and turned around, and there was Sean with two other boys from school, coming his way. Fast.

But Jay? When he heard that voice call out his

name? He didn't stop, didn't turn to look, didn't react at all. Jay kept walking straight ahead, just some kid in a red sweatshirt. And a second later he took a sharp left and went through the open doorway of a huge entertainment store.

So by the time Mr. and Mrs. Grayson turned around to see who had called out to one of their sons, they believed they were looking at Jay, wearing his blue Cubs cap, talking to some redheaded kid and two other boys.

But they didn't see Ray's red hoodie anywhere. And that worried them. Losing sight of a boy at the mall made all their warning bells ring.

Sean got within range of Ray and called, "Hey, how's it goin'?"

He smiled and said, "Pretty good." Which was a lie.

As the four boys formed up into a loose circle, Sean nodded toward the other two guys. "That's Ed—you met him at lunch today. And this other loser is Kent."

Kent punched Sean on the arm and said, "*You're* the loser." Then to Ray he said, "Hi."

Ray nodded, then looked over his shoulder and saw that his parents had stopped, and now his dad was hurrying back toward him. Ray guessed he had about twenty seconds before impact. So he said, "Listen, that's my dad coming at us. I've gotta go get some shoes."

Sean said, "Cleats?"

Ray looked confused. "Cleats? Why?"

Sean said, "For soccer. James said you're gonna be at practice on Monday."

Ray nodded and said, "Right. On Monday. Yeah, I need . . . cleats." And he thought, *Jay's gonna pay for this.*

Sean said, "Check out the Adidas. They cost a lot, but they're worth it."

Ray nodded again. "Adidas. Right. Well, listen, I gotta go with my dad. See you guys later."

"Yeah," Sean said. "See ya."

And the three boys turned and headed back the way they had come.

Four seconds later Ray's dad was next to him, a worried look on his face. "Where's Ray?" he asked.

Ray jerked a thumb left toward the entertainment store. "Probably in there."

And Jay, who had been watching from behind a big cardboard cutout of a drooling alien, stepped into the open, smiled, and waved at his dad.

His dad did not wave back. Or smile.

Jay hurried out of the store and said, "What's going on?"

Dad said, "What's going on is, until we get back to the car, both of you are walking right behind Mom and me, got it? No ducking into stores, no stopping to talk, no wandering away on your own. Now march."

Jay said, "Dad, we're twelve years old."

Their dad nodded. "Which is why you're going to do exactly what I say. March."

So the boys marched.

They got to where their mom was waiting, and after they all started walking along together, Ray said to Jay, "Hey, guess what, Ray?"

And Jay said, "What?"

And Ray said, "I'm gonna get some cleats at the shoe store."

"Cleats?" said Jay. "How come?"

"Because I'm going to soccer practice. After school. On Monday," Ray said. "But maybe you already knew that—*Ray.*"

And their mom, who was only five feet ahead of them now, turned her head to look at Ray and said, "Soccer? That's great, Jay." And then looking at Jay, she asked, "How about you, Ray? Aren't you on the team?"

And Jay said, "Um, no. Just . . . Jay."

She said, "But I'm sure you're as good at soccer as Jay is. You should join the team too."

Speaking for Ray, Jay said, "I don't like soccer, Mom. So I'll just watch. From the bleachers."

"Well, I don't want you coming home alone," Mom said, "so you're going to have to find something to do after school. And I still think you should try out for soccer. It's a great sport."

And when she turned away, Ray said, "Yeah, Ray, it's a *great* sport." And as he said "great," he slugged Jay on the arm. Hard.

And then he whispered, "Anything else you want to tell me, any other little surprises?"

Jay shook his head. "Nope," he whispered back. "Melissa thinks Jay is kind of a dork now, and on Monday Jay is going to soccer practice after school. That's all. Not bad for one day's work, huh?"

And for that little joke, Jay got another punch on the arm. From Ray. Dressed as Jay.

And when Ray punched him that second time, Jay didn't yell, "Ow!" and grab his arm like he usually would have. Because at this moment, that would have meant getting *himself* in trouble.

So at the shoe store, Ray, dressed as Jay, picked out some soccer cleats. For the real Jay. And Jay, dressed as Ray, picked out a great new pair of sneakers. For the real Ray.

Except on Monday, when the real Ray wore his very own new sneakers to school, everyone would think they belonged to Jay. And he'd be carrying the real Jay's new soccer cleats. For after school. Because on Monday, the real Ray would be going to school as the fake Jay. Again.

That is, if the Grayson brothers could get through Saturday and Sunday without strangling each other.

CHAPTER 12

FLIP FLOP FLIP

Saturday was a perfect September day—blue sky, low humidity, about seventy degrees. And that meant it was time to do yard work. And housework. And more unpacking.

And that meant that Ray and Jay had to coordinate their whereabouts so they wouldn't be outside in the same area at the same moment. Which turned out to be important.

Because while Ray was mowing the front lawn, a guy from his Thursday gym class rode by on his bike. He waved and yelled, "Hey—I live on the next block! See you round."

And while Jay was stacking the third bundle of flattened cardboard boxes in the recycling pile at the front curb, a girl he remembered from music class waved at him out the window of a passing car.

It was a long, busy morning, and there was still a lot left to do. But while they were eating lunch at about one thirty, their dad said, "How about we knock off for the afternoon, walk over to the park, and play some baseball?"

Which sounded great. Except for the rule about not being visible in the same place at the time. Ray and Jay went up to their room, and after a short argument, they agreed to flip a coin to see who got to go. And Ray won the toss.

So Jay had to stay home and hide in the house. Plus work on the social studies report, because that was the excuse he gave for not wanting to go play baseball. Which was one more lie—a big one. To spend a sunny afternoon researching the cultures of Mesopotamia was not what he wanted to do. And after about an hour of off-and-on work, he lay down on his bed and took a long nap.

The best part of Jay's Saturday was waking up from his nap to discover that a big bag of Chinese food had just been delivered, and dinner was served.

He sat down at the kitchen table and reached for his favorite Chinese food—the fortune cookie. Jay knew he was supposed to wait and have it last, but he never did.

His mom said, "So what's your fortune?"

"It says, 'If your path becomes difficult, never despair.'"

His dad nodded. "Good advice. Please pass the spring rolls."

The whole family was hungry, so there wasn't much talk for the next few minutes. And when the phone rang, no one jumped to get it because every mouth was full. Mr. Grayson answered it on the fourth ring.

"Hello?"

He listened a moment, then gave the handset to Jay. "It's someone named Alex."

Jay gulped down a bite of chicken and said, "Alex—hi."

"Hi, Jay. You eating? 'Cause I can call back."

"No, it's okay."

"I wanted to see if you're up for a stick session. At the rink tomorrow."

"A stick session?" Jay asked.

"Yeah, it's free skate time, except you can have sticks and pucks. And you have to wear a helmet. You want to come?"

"Yeah, I do," Jay said, "except I don't have a helmet. Or a stick."

"I've got tons of that stuff," Alex said. "So

we'll pick you up about one o'clock, okay? My dad's driving."

"Sounds great," Jay said, "but hang on a second."

He covered the mouthpiece of the portable phone with his hand, looked at his mom and dad, and said, "Alex is in my homeroom, and he wants me to go skating with him tomorrow about one o'clock—is that okay?"

His mom said, "What about your social studies report? I looked at that assignment, and you didn't get much done this afternoon. I think you'd better not."

"But it's not due until Wednesday, Mom."

She shook her head. "Sunday afternoon is for homework—you know that. And that report's nowhere near done."

Jay turned away from the table and talked quickly into the phone. "Listen, Alex, I'll call you back in about five minutes, okay?"

"Sure," he said. "Talk to you later. 'Bye."

"'Bye." Jay pushed the off button and put the phone on the table.

His mom shook her head. "I am not changing my mind, so you can call that boy back right now."

Jay knew that tone of voice. "Fine," he snapped, and he pushed back from the table, grabbed the phone, stomped up to his room, and slammed the door. He flopped onto his bed and was all set to call Alex back, when Ray burst into the room and grabbed the phone out of his hands.

"What are you doing?" Jay said.

Ray sat on the edge of the bed. "Listen," he said, "I know this stinks for you, but I asked Mom if I could go skating with Alex. Instead of you. Since I'm all caught up on my homework and everything. And she said I could. So I'm gonna call him back, okay?"

Jay sat up on the bed and stared at his brother. "*You*? He invited *me* to go skating, not you. And the only reason you don't have homework is because *I'm* the one who's really going to school."

"Don't be stupid," Ray said. "Who talked about hockey with Alex all through homeroom on Thursday? Me. So he's asking *me* to go skating just as much as he's asking you. And tomorrow, all I have to do is meet Alex at his car out in the driveway. You stay out of sight, and he'll never know the difference. Besides, I'm tons better at skating than you are."

Jay wanted to grab the phone back from Ray and stuff it up his left nostril. But then a better idea popped into his mind.

"You know what? Here's how it's gonna work: *You* pretend to be me and you stay here and do homework. And as far as Mom's concerned, it'll be *you* going to the ice rink. Except it'll be me. And it's fair because *I'm* the one who stayed in the house all afternoon while you went and played baseball today. So tomorrow *I* get to go skating—and that's the only way that's fair. Right?"

Ray didn't answer.

"*Right?*" Jay said. Louder.

"Fine," said Ray, his teeth clenched. He whipped the phone at Jay's leg. "I hope you have a rotten time." And he got up and stomped out of their room.

As Jay picked the phone up off the floor, his leg hurt a little. But he didn't care one bit, because *he* was going skating.

It really was the fairest solution, and Ray knew that, so by bedtime on Saturday, he and Jay were on speaking terms again. And by Sunday afternoon, they had the switch all set.

Jay was wearing Ray's red hoodie again, plus his Cardinals hat—the same outfit he'd worn to the mall on Friday night. And Ray was wearing one of Jay's blue shirts and a pair of his jeans. Jay had also made sure to grab the skates that were marked with Ray's initials.

A few minutes before one, Jay was waiting by the front door with the skates, and Ray was standing off in the doorway of the dining room.

"Listen," Ray said, "be sure to ask Alex how to do crossovers—you still don't do that right, and it really helps you build up speed."

Jay nodded and said, "Yeah, I'll ask him. And next time we'll both go with him." Which was a very nice thing to say to a brother who had to stay home.

A horn honked from the curb, and Jay yelled out, "They're here—I'm going now."

His dad muted the baseball game and called from the living room, "Have a good time, and be sure to pay for your own admission, okay?"

Jay pulled the door open. "I will, Dad."

Mom called from the upstairs office, "Wait a second, honey, I'm coming down."

She came and looked out through the screen door, then waved toward the car. "You be a good guest, all right? And no rough stuff."

Jay said, "I know, Mom, I know," and he pushed the screen door open to leave.

Ray said, "See you, Ray," and turned to walk upstairs. To do homework.

Without looking back, Jay said, "Later, Jay," and started out the door.

"Oh—Ray?" his mom said. "Be sure—" But she didn't finish that sentence.

Because as she said the name "Ray," both boys turned their heads to her and said, "What?" In unison.

She looked from one boy to the other, and then back. Then her eyes flashed, and she grabbed Jay by the arm and pulled him back into the front hallway.

"Very cute," she said.

Jay looked surprised. "What?" he said. "What are you talking about?"

She glared at Jay. "Do we need to do the freckle-check here?" Turning to the boy by the stairs, she said, "Do we—*Ray*?"

There was no way out. Their mom knew they had tried to trick her, and that was that.

So Ray immediately said, "I was just trying to be nice, Mom. Because Jay didn't get to play baseball yesterday. And I wanted to help with his report."

She shook her head. "No. Jay has to stay and do his own work."

Ray said, "But . . . like, I can still go, right? Please?"

She paused a second, then said, "Yes, but only because I'm sure Alex's father had to drive out of his way to come pick you up. But both of you can count on hearing more about this. Now—Ray, get going. And Jay, upstairs."

So Jay took off the Cardinals hat, handed Ray his own skates, peeled off Ray's red sweatshirt and gave it to him, and went upstairs. To work on the social studies report.

And a second later he heard the screen door slam.

But as Jay went into his room, sat down at his desk, and flipped his notebook open, he wasn't mad at Ray for taking his place at the last second. Alex wanted to skate with a friend. And Ray was an excellent skater. They'd both have a good time.

Still, as Jay stared at the assignment sheet and looked at the due date again, he realized that after he did a great job on this report, who would be turning it in on Wednesday? Ray.

Because Wednesday was not going to be a Jay day at school. Wednesday was going to be a Ray day.

And to Jay, it was starting to feel like every day was a Ray day.

And it didn't feel good. In fact, it felt a little like . . . despair.

CHAPTER 13

TOP SECRET

On Monday morning Ray dragged Jay out of his bed at seven thirty, and then hurried him along so they could leave together for school twenty minutes early. Which Jay didn't like. That meant *he* had to hide out that much longer in the cardboard igloo in the garage. At least Jay wouldn't have to listen to Ray tell him again how much fun the skating had been. Because Jay was fed up with everything that Ray had to say. About anything.

But Ray didn't care what Jay thought. Ray was a man with a Monday morning mission. He had to find Melissa before homeroom and then try to repair the damage Jay had done during science class on Friday.

Ray got to school before the buses, and he took a position inside the wide front doors of the school. He had a clear view of the whole unloading area.

Spotting Melissa was easy. She came down the steps of bus number three, a soft blue hat and scarf framing her face. And when Ray saw her smile at a friend, he remembered how it had felt to have that smile aimed his way.

In addition to being pretty, Melissa was apparently popular. The moment she got off the bus, four other girls flocked around her, and together the group made their way toward Ray. And as they came through the second set of glass doors, he waited, waited, and then made his move, walking so that he crossed her path.

"Melissa—hi."

Melissa turned her head, saw who it was, smiled slightly, and kept walking. It was not the same kind of smile she'd given Ray on Thursday. And she didn't even say hi.

He fell in walking beside her.

"Hey, Melissa . . . can I talk to you a second?" Ray was not at all shy about speaking to a girl, even if other girls were listening. Which they were.

Melissa kept walking toward the sixth-grade hall. "Why?" she asked. "Do you . . . like my shirt?"

A couple of the other girls giggled, but the joke was lost on Ray. Jay had not shared the full details of his desperate attempt to chat with this girl on Friday.

Ray shook his head and said, "No, it's just that . . . well, it's sort of . . . sad. Except, I don't know if you can keep a secret."

Ray was using his vast experience with girls. Because he had discovered that few girls can resist hearing about something that might be tragic. Even fewer girls can resist the chance to learn some private information. And combining these elements was a guaranteed girl-stopper.

And sure enough, Melissa stopped walking and turned to look at Ray with renewed interest.

Ray looked at Melissa's friends, and then at the floor.

Melissa got the message.

"Listen, guys," she said, "I'll see you in homeroom, okay?" And the group moved on, whispering to one another and peeking back over their shoulders at Ray.

Melissa stood facing Ray next to the lockers just inside the sixth-grade hall. Ray could see the questions there in her eyes—which were a nice greenish gray color.

Now came the tricky part. Because Ray had no idea what he was going to say to Melissa.

Some quick ideas popped into his head. *I could say I fell onto my head Friday morning, and that's why*

I acted so goofy in science class. Or . . . I could say sometimes I just get flustered when I talk to girls, especially really cute ones—that sounds good. Or I could say that my pet hamster died Friday morning, and I was a mess all day . . . but I didn't want anyone to know I was upset, because that might make me seem like I was wimpy or something—and that's something sad plus something secret.

But standing there looking into Melissa's face, Ray suddenly felt helpless. He knew he didn't want to make up some story. She really did seem like a nice girl, someone he could like. A lot.

Because if he made up one story, then he'd have to make up another, to cover the first one. And then another story, and another. Because the truth about him and Jay was going to come out. Soon. Like, on Friday. And that was just four more days. And deep down, Ray felt pretty sure that if he stood here right now and told a long string of lies, he could forget about being friends with Melissa. Or any of her buddies.

So Ray took a deep breath, looked right into the girl's eyes, and said, "That kid you talked to in science on Friday? That was Jay. Jay Grayson."

Melissa scrunched her eyebrows together. "Right—Jay. Which is you . . . Jay."

Ray shook his head. "I'm Ray. And I met you on Thursday when we got assigned to be lab partners. And Jay is . . . he's my twin brother. And the school lost my records. They don't even know there is a Ray Grayson. So Jay and I have been switching off, going to school every other day. And we both use his name—Jay. So . . . that's the secret part of what I had to tell you. And the sad part is, that you had to talk to *him* on Friday. Instead of me. Because sometimes Jay can be sort of . . . lame."

Melissa's face was hard to read—disbelief, fascination, confusion. But mostly fascination. Because the girl had an imagination. She didn't believe what Ray was saying, but she was willing to be convinced.

She said, "So . . . like, one of you stays home? Every school day?"

Ray nodded. Then he explained about using their hideout in the garage. "And after my folks leave for work, the guy at home just goes back into the house. Grabs some food, watches a movie, sleeps, reads—you know, stay-at-home stuff."

Melissa wrinkled her nose. "You're just making all this up. I mean, I could tell you the same story, that *I* have a twin sister. Named Clarissa. And *she's* the one who thought you were . . . lame. On Friday."

"Well, yeah, you could say the same thing," Ray

said. "But, c'mon, you talked to Jay, right? And now you're talking to me, Ray." He gave her his brightest, most charming smile. "You can tell that I'm not the same as him, can't you? Except for the way I look, I mean."

Melissa looked into Ray's face, saw his quiet, confident smile, saw him meet her questioning gaze without a trace of anxiety. And Ray could see the change in her eyes. Because she could tell. She *knew* he wasn't Jay. At all.

Almost whispering, she said, "So you . . . you really *are* twins. And the other one—Jay? He's at home, right? Hiding out. That is so *cool!*"

Ray nodded, "Yeah, I know. Except you have to keep this a total secret, okay? I mean, like, completely. We're not telling the school about it until Friday. And we're gonna get in some real trouble about this. But we had to try it out, to see what it would be like to be on our own, instead of always being twins. We had to."

As Ray talked, the look on Melissa's face kept changing. Because now she was also worried for him. About the trouble. And there was also a trace of admiration, because the danger made Ray seem like sort of an outlaw, a rebel, a risk taker. And that touch of adventure was irresistible.

Ray saw all of this in her face, and it brought out the actor in him.

With a faraway look in his eyes, he said, "Yeah, we're making every day count. Because the hammer's gonna come down on us pretty hard."

Melissa's eyes were wide. "You'd better be careful," she whispered.

Ray paused dramatically, searching her eyes. And he said, "But I can trust you, right?"

She nodded. "Yes. Yes, you can."

"Good," Ray said. "Listen, I'll see you in science, okay? And maybe at lunchtime, too."

She nodded. "At lunchtime, too."

"Good. See you later, Melissa."

"See you . . . Jay." And she gave Ray one of her million-dollar smiles.

Walking toward his homeroom, Ray felt like he was the king of Ohio.

At the start of math class fifteen minutes later, Ray spotted the girl Jay had told him about. And during attendance he learned her name—Julie Parkman. Ray didn't think she was anywhere near as cute as Melissa, but he smiled at her anyway, and he got a chance to talk with her after class. And Ray was friendly with her—not like *he* would have been, of course. He was friendly with Julie in a

Jayish sort of way—a little stiff, sort of reserved, kind of unsure of himself. Because Ray didn't want to spoil things for Jay by having this girl think that Jay was going to be like him. Because *that* wasn't gonna happen.

And as Ray said, "Well, see you later," to Julie, he wasn't worried about Melissa finding out that he'd been talking to some other girl, not at all. Because now he could explain that he talked to her just to be nice to his brother. Which was true.

As Ray headed down the hall to the music room, he still felt like the king of Ohio, plus he felt like he could have won the Boston Marathon. And then climbed Mount Everest.

Ray sang his heart out during music class, and when Mr. Parnell asked for volunteers to join the sixth-grade chorus, Ray was the first boy to raise his hand. He felt like he could have stood up and sung a solo right then and there.

In fact, Ray's whole day was great, especially the quiet talk he had with Melissa next to the foursquare courts during lunch recess, and double-especially the time he spent sitting next to her during science class.

And even during soccer practice after school, Ray felt terrific. He did his best to pretend that soccer wasn't just a lot of semipointless running around on a big field. He ran hard and tried to look like he knew what he was doing. He even scraped up his knee as he made a sliding tackle during scrimmage, and didn't complain about it to anyone. And Ray did all that extra-hard work at soccer practice for Jay's sake, out of gratitude.

Because if Jay hadn't been a complete doofus with Melissa on Friday, then Ray wouldn't have had to tell her the truth on Monday morning. And telling her the truth had made Ray feel so good. It had made Melissa feel good too, to be trusted like that.

And even though Melissa was just one person out of so many others at the school, with her knowing his secret, Ray felt much more like himself all day long—even when kids called him Jay.

Because Melissa Rollins *knew* who he was. She knew it.

And she definitely liked him—*him*, Ray Grayson.

CHAPTER 14

NOT SO SECRET

By lunchtime on Monday, Melissa was having trouble. And the trouble was this secret she knew. Because Jay wasn't Jay at all, not today. He was Jay's twin brother, Ray. And actually, Ray was the boy she'd started to get a crush on way back on Thursday. Because *that* day, Jay had really been Ray. So there wasn't just one cute new boy at Taft Elementary, there were *two*, and they were exactly alike. And to be the only other person in the whole school who knew about this? It was like no secret Melissa had ever known before. And she was dying to tell someone. Anyone.

Except . . . she had promised Ray she would keep the secret. And she really wanted to. She did. Really.

But for Melissa, this secret was like that twenty-dollar bill her aunt had given her for her birthday. She knew she should have taken that money and tucked it away somewhere safe, like the bank. But instead, she took it somewhere else. Like, to the mall.

And today, right now? The school cafeteria was like the mall. It was the perfect place to spend a secret. So Melissa began shopping for a pair of ears. Ears that belonged to someone she could trust. Someone who wasn't a blabbermouth. As she dropped off her tray after eating, Melissa looked around, and then waved to her friend Caroline and motioned that she should come over—quick.

And standing against the wall under the food-groups poster, the two girls shared forty-five seconds of furious whispering and nodding. And when it was over, Caroline's mouth was hanging wide open. Because she was in on the secret. She knew that Jay had an identical twin brother named Ray who was coming to school every other day, and that these two adorably cute brothers had all the teachers duped into thinking they were the same kid. And of course, the last thing Melissa said was, "You have to promise me that you won't tell anybody, okay? Like, nobody. Promise?"

And Caroline promised to keep the secret.

Outside on the playground five minutes later,

Caroline saw Ray and Melissa talking next to the foursquare courts, saw them nodding and smiling at each other—and it seemed so romantic. Almost dangerous. Because that boy was sort of like a spy. Or a secret agent. And suddenly Caroline wished she could tell her best friend Brianna about this. And that's when Caroline decided that even though she had promised Melissa to keep the Ray and Jay thing secret, that didn't mean she couldn't tell Brianna. Because Caroline knew she could trust Brianna. So on the way back to their lockers after recess, Brianna heard the whole story.

"He has a *twin*?" Brianna gasped. "That new kid? In my math class? And the twin told Melissa? Because he *likes* her? That's so *sweet*, don't you think? And don't worry. I won't tell *anyone*. Really. I promise."

And Brianna didn't tell a single soul for a whole seven minutes. And as Brianna whispered to her friend Lori what Caroline had told her about what Melissa said that this boy named Ray had told *her*, did Brianna think she wasn't keeping Caroline's secret? Not at all. Because Brianna knew that Lori was a girl who knew how to keep her mouth shut.

And all during science class, as Melissa and the boy known as Jay sat at the same lab table, Brianna and Lori kept a close eye on them. And whenever the boy and Melissa would whisper to each other, Brianna and Lori would look at each other with a wink. Or a nod. Or a smile. Because that boy at table nine was *not* who he appeared to be.

The secret news about the Grayson twins was shared three or four more times on Monday afternoon. And after school, as bus number four rumbled out of the parking lot, a girl named Jenny whispered to her best friend LeeAnn, "If you promise to keep this a secret, I know something about that new kid in our social studies class, the boy named Jay."

LeeAnn nodded and whispered back, "You mean, how he's a twin, and how he and his brother have been tricking the whole school? I heard about it from Carrie during gym. Isn't it *amazing*?"

And just then, Jenny grabbed LeeAnn's shoulder and pointed out the window at a boy walking along the sidewalk on Baker Street. "Ooh, look! Look!" she said. "Right there—that's him! That's the boy!"

And LeeAnn jumped to her feet and yelled out the bus window, "Hi, Jay!"

The boy jerked his head toward the bus with a startled look, then smiled and waved. Both girls collapsed onto the bus seat in a fit of giggles.

And as Jenny looked back over her shoulder, she whispered, "Is that really Jay? Or is that, like, the *other* one?"

LeeAnn shrugged. "That's the thing—there's no way to tell!"

And the girls kept on giggling.

CHAPTER 15

RAYNESS

It was Tuesday afternoon, and as he trudged along the hallway, Jay was wishing for a fire drill. Or an emergency all-school assembly. Or a sudden attack of giant man-eating alien insects— anything that might delay the beginning of science class. Because he was going to have to spend another whole period sitting next to Melissa. And he thought, *Since Ray was here yesterday, and since he told me that he's got everything patched up with her, now the girl's expecting someone like him again. Not someone like me.*

Girls had been on Jay's mind all day anyway. Ever since homeroom, he'd had this funny feeling. He felt like girls kept looking at him—not staring or anything, more like a peek here, a glance there. And Jay wasn't used to that. Not unless he was hanging out with Ray. When the two of them were together, it wasn't unusual for girls to notice them, not at all. Because Jay knew that he and Ray were both kind of good-looking. He knew that. And when they were together, then the twins thing kicked in. Girls noticed. Along with everyone else.

But this felt different. Like they were looking at *him*. And even whispering to each other. About *him*. Weird.

So all morning Jay had just put it out of his mind, had tried not to think about it. If girls wanted to look at him and whisper about him, there wasn't much he could do about it. Girls. A major mystery.

Although . . . Tuesday morning's math class with Julie Parkman had gone surprisingly well. He had said hi to her before class, and she had smiled at him. And at the end of class, they had walked halfway to the art room together. And they had even talked a little. Mostly about math, but still, he had been talking to a girl for almost two minutes. And during that whole time, Jay had felt calm and steady, very much himself. Julie had seemed like an easy girl to talk to. No pressure.

But with Melissa it was different. And as he neared the science room, Jay's armpits were damp and his hands felt sweaty too. And he said to himself, *I'll just have to pretend I'm like Ray, that's all.*

Sort of smooth and charming. And easygoing. Like Ray.

Jay peeked into the room and saw that Melissa hadn't come to class yet. So he hurried over to table number nine, took his seat, and rummaged around in his book bag for the homework. But he didn't feel like Ray at all. Jay felt like himself, awkward and scared.

He was scared because he was lacking one important bit of information: Jay didn't know that Melissa knew about the secret. And Jay didn't know because Ray hadn't told him. And Ray hadn't told because Ray felt pretty sure that Jay would have gotten mad about him telling someone—even someone as cute as Melissa. And that's why Ray had also asked Melissa not to let Jay know that she knew. About him being a twin.

So as Jay was dreading having to be like Ray for a whole period, Melissa was thrilled about having a whole period to get a close look at the real Jay Grayson. And the fact that he didn't know that she knew who he really was? That was a perfectly delicious secret.

And Melissa didn't know that while she was sitting with Jay, three or four other girls in the science room were also going to be watching and listening. Secretly.

When Melissa came rushing in just as the bell rang and sat down next to him, Jay still had no idea what do. Or what to say. Or how to act.

Be like Ray, he told himself. *Be like Ray.*

So Jay put a Ray-like smile on his face, looked sideways at Melissa, and said, "Hey, how's it going?"

And Melissa thought, *He's trying to be like his brother—that is so* cute! So she gave him a huge smile, and she said, "Good, really good."

Jay nodded toward his homework sheet in that offhanded way he'd seen Ray nod so many times, and he said, "Pretty tough assignment. What did you get for the third problem?"

Melissa smiled at him again as she pulled a yellow three-ring binder from her book bag, opened it on the desk, flipped to the divider marked HOME-WORK, turned three or four pages, then ran her index finger down the worksheet. And she said, "Nitrogen, right? Because of the five electrons."

Jay stared at Melissa's fingernail, completely distracted by the remains of some hot-pink nail polish. But he managed to say, "Yeah, nitrogen. That's what I got too." And he said it like Ray would have said it—or the way he imagined Ray would have said it.

And again, Melissa gave him a really big smile.

And as Jay smiled back, he thought, *Oh yeah, I'm nailin' this. I am way cool—no, I'm Ray cool.*

Science class went zipping along in a cheerful blur, and Jay had never had so much fun talking with a girl in his life. He felt like he sort of had an actual girlfriend. And as they began work on the new lab assignment, Jay relaxed. He was smooth, at ease, funny, and very charming. Very Ray. And Melissa? As far as Jay could tell, the girl was eating it up. With a spoon. She couldn't stop smiling at him. And the more Jay tried to be like Ray, the more she smiled.

Jay had to admit that Melissa seemed a lot cuter today than he'd thought she was on Friday. But still nowhere near as cute as Julie Parkman. But there would be time for her. Because this little adventure in Rayness was giving Jay all kinds of ideas. It was suddenly obvious that he could be much cooler and smoother than he had ever imagined possible. Jay thought, *When it comes to girls, Jay is the new Ray—new and improved. And the school year is just beginning!*

When science class ended, Jay smiled at Melissa and said, "See you tomorrow." And he wished that were true. But it wasn't. Because tomorrow, the other Jay would be sitting at table nine.

Still, as he walked out into the crowded hallway

and caught up with James for the walk to gym class, Jay felt like he was on top of the world.

And he was especially looking forward to soccer practice after school. He couldn't wait to show James how the *real* Jay Grayson played the game.

CHAPTER 16

THE LITTLE THINGS

During his second lap around the big oval track behind the school, Jay remembered exactly why he had never wanted to be on a soccer team: too much running—*way* too much. But still, he felt like he was doing okay. He was having no trouble keeping up with James. *Not bad for my first practice*, Jay told himself.

The two of them were actually leading the pack, a good thirty yards out in front of the rest of the guys, and that made Jay feel good too. Because when it came to sports, he didn't have to try to be like Ray. Ray had to try to be like him.

During the first lap, he and James had talked a little as they jogged, mostly about baseball. James was a big Cleveland Indians fan, and Jay liked the Colorado Rockies, and neither team was even in the wild-card race. So they'd had fun comparing

best and worst pitchers, then best and worst batters, then best and worst pennant races all around both leagues. The conversation went back and forth until they began to need all their air for running. And the second trip around the track was mostly quiet.

But as they began the third lap, James looked over at Jay and said, "How's your knee?"

"My knee?"

"Yeah," James said, "from that scrape yesterday. You were really limping for a while. Looked bad—blood on your sock and everything? Thought you'd have it taped up today."

"Oh—that," Jay said, and he pretended to breathe with extra effort for five or ten seconds, giving himself time to think. Then he said, "Wasn't as bad as it looked. And stuff like that? I heal up really fast. Almost can't see it now."

James glanced at him again and nodded, but he didn't reply.

Another thirty yards or so bounced by, and then James said, "You met my little brothers yet?"

Jay said, "Nope—just moved here, remember?"

James said, "Thought you might have noticed them around school. They look a lot like me. Robert and Edward. They're twins, completely identical."

Jay jerked his head sideways to look at James and almost stumbled. But James was running, eyes straight ahead, face expressionless.

Jay kept his voice as even as possible. "Twins, huh? So what's that like?"

James took about ten strides before he answered. "Kinda fun. They're good little guys. And no one can tell which is which, sometimes not even our parents. But I always know."

Jay glanced sideways again. "How's that work?"

"Not sure," James said. "I can just tell. That they're different. Different people."

After a few more strides, he added, "And I see a lot of little things. 'Cause I'm good at noticing stuff. That's what the art teacher says. That I'm good at seeing. Like an artist, I guess."

"So you're good at art? Like, drawing and painting?" Jay wanted to change the subject. "I'm lousy at that stuff," he said. "Can you draw faces? I can never draw faces."

But James stayed on his point. "Because with Edward and Robert? The thing is, they only *look* identical. They're not really the same at all. Not if you notice little things. Or even big things. Like a scraped knee."

Jay stopped running, just stopped. And so did

James. Then they stepped off the track and stood on the grass, panting, while the other twelve guys went huffing past.

"So . . . ," Jay said, "like, when did you know?"

James grinned. "For sure? Today, when we started running. No scratches on your knee. Plus, you're a lot faster, and you've got a whole different stride. And you don't swing your elbows out like a chicken when you run. Which is what the other guy does."

"His name's Ray," said Jay. "Can you believe that? My parents named us Jay and Ray."

From across the field a sharp blast from the coach's whistle got both boys back onto the track. And while they finished the third lap, Jay told the whole story. And he made James promise not to tell anyone else.

As they pulled on some yellow vests to get ready for a scrimmage, Jay said, "And listen, don't tell Ray, either, okay? 'Cause he didn't want to try this in the first place. And it would just make him nervous if he knew. That someone else knew about us."

And James smiled and nodded. "No problem. I won't tell him—as long as *you* don't tell my little brothers one word about this, okay?"

They both laughed a little at that, then James

added, "It's really cool, y'know, what you guys are doing. If I could ditch school every other day, I would totally do that."

Jay nodded, and he wanted to say, *But really, that's not what this is about, like staying home or tricking everybody. Me and Ray, we're just trying to do a few things on our own. And the best part isn't staying home. It's stuff at school—stuff like this, right now.*

But Jay didn't say that. Because most kids wouldn't understand. It was a twins thing.

So all he said was, "Yeah, but this whole deal is weird, too. And when it ends—who knows what'll happen? 'Cause at the end of this week, we're stopping it. Friday's gonna be quite a day."

The coach started calling out positions, so their conversation was over. But that phrase stuck in Jay's head, and he said it again to himself: *Friday's gonna be quite a day.*

Except Jay was wrong about that. Because other forces were in motion at Taft Elementary School.

And Jay and Ray had no idea what was coming. Or when.

But something was coming. And soon.

Soon.

CHAPTER 17

DETECTION

The door of Mrs. Cardiff's room was always open. And there was a sign above that open doorway: SCHOOL NURSE.

Much smaller than a classroom, the nurse's office was not a fancy place: charts and posters on the painted yellow walls, one pale oak desk with a rolling chair, three filing cabinets, one low vinyl cot, one folding privacy screen, one scale, and three different-size chairs for different-size visitors. Also, the nurse's room was the only office in the school with its own private bathroom.

Mrs. Cardiff was an excellent school nurse, which means that she was part mother hen, part educator, and part detective. And at times she also acted as a child advocate, as a parent-teacher arbitrator, and when needed, as a first responder.

And when she had to, she could summon the

full authority of the Ohio Department of Health with one phone call. Nobody messed with Emma Cardiff, RN.

Mrs. Cardiff spent a good part of every day standing outside her open doorway, which was at the intersection of the main hallways near the entrance of the school. She watched the children arrive in the morning, she watched them go to and from the cafeteria during the lunch periods, and she watched them hurry homeward at the end of the day.

If a child seemed unusually thin or especially heavy, she took notice. If a child seemed overly tired or oddly energetic, she got on that case. If a child was limping or squinting or scratching or coughing, the nurse looked into the matter. She rarely missed a clue, because she wanted each of the kids here to be as happy and comfortable as possible.

At the start of every year Mrs. Cardiff paid special attention to the eyes and the ears of the kids. She had some students on a "watch list" so she could follow up on them each fall. She had gotten some referrals from teachers for kids who might need hearing or vision testing. And then there were the transfer kids, the ones who had moved into town over the summer. Those children always got some special attention from Mrs. Cardiff.

And that box Jay had seen in his homeroom? The one with the student folders—the folders that Ray thought had been tucked away for the rest of the year? They hadn't been filed away at all. All the boxes from every grade had been stacked in a small storage area next to the nurse's room. And like a detective hunting for clues, Mrs. Cardiff had been carefully working her way through those files for the past several days.

As usual, she had started with the sixth graders, glancing through every file for new health notes, and she had pulled out the files of the kids on her special watch list. And she had also set aside the files of all the new transfers.

Then she did that same kind of search through the file boxes for each of the other grades. And when she had all the file folders she wanted to examine pulled from the boxes into a tall stack on her desk, she began carefully reading each file again, starting with the sixth graders.

And that's why on Wednesday morning, twenty minutes before the first buses arrived, the school nurse opened up a thick, bright blue student folder labeled, "Grayson, Jay Ray."

Less than ten minutes later, Mrs. Cardiff called an emergency meeting with the principal and with Jay's homeroom teacher, Mrs. Lane.

Because it didn't take a Sherlock Holmes to see that there was something wrong with the Grayson file—very, very wrong.

CHAPTER 18

THE SITUATION

The principal, Mrs. Karen Lonsdale, sat behind her desk in her office, the Grayson file open in front of her. She was holding two small photographs, one in each hand. She looked from one picture to the other, and then back again, and then she glanced up into the face of Mrs. Lane. "And only one of these boys has been at school? Since last Tuesday?"

Mrs. Lane nodded.

Looking at the nurse, Mrs. Lonsdale said, "Have you tried to reach the parents yet?"

Mrs. Cardiff shook her head and said, "I wanted to speak with both of you first. There's nothing in the file to indicate it, but this could be a divorce situation, and maybe there's a custody issue we don't know about. I don't see any record of either parent actually coming to the school yet, so I don't know what to think."

The principal said, "So . . . should we call the child welfare agency? Or the police? Because the one thing we know for sure is that we have a missing child. Jay Grayson has been coming to school for a week now, and we've heard nothing about this other brother from the boy or from the parents. No note, no explanation of any kind. What's the other child's name?"

"Ray," Mrs. Cardiff said. "One is Jay and the other one's Ray."

Turning to Mrs. Lane, the principal frowned and said, "What I want to know is, why didn't you spot this when you read through your student files last week?"

Mrs. Lane was upset. "Well, I . . . I know I looked through all the folders, but I didn't really study every file, and I guess—"

The nurse interrupted. "I almost didn't spot it myself, Karen. One boy is named Jay Ray, and the other is Ray Jay, and all the photos in that file look exactly alike. Two files got stuffed into an envelope by someone in Colorado, and when it arrived here in the mail, it looked like we were getting one new student. The district secretary didn't catch it, or the district attendance officer, or our own school secretary—no one caught the mistake. And right now, we know that we are one student short. So the question isn't, 'Who should have seen this?' The question is, 'Where's the missing boy?'"

The principal nodded in agreement, and Jay's homeroom teacher smiled at the nurse, grateful for the support.

The principal said, "So again, who should we call about this?"

Mrs. Lane shrugged.

Not Mrs. Cardiff. She never shrugged. She always had a positive idea about what to do next, and this Grayson business was no exception.

She sat up straight on the edge of her chair and said, "There might be a very simple explanation about why the other twin hasn't been coming, so we don't want to overreact. First I think we need to talk to Jay, the boy who's at school. I'm beginning the hearing tests today, so I could call him to my office during homeroom. The audiologist won't arrive until later, but I can just talk with him a little, in a non-threatening way. And based on what we learn, then I suggest that we call the parents. And if for some reason the parents are not cooperative, then we can involve the authorities. Does that sound like a good way forward?"

The principal and the homeroom teacher looked at each other, and both nodded in agreement.

Mrs. Lonsdale stood up, closed the blue file folder, and handed it across her desk to the nurse. "All right, then. That's what we'll do. And for now, let's keep this matter to ourselves, understood?"

Mrs. Lane and Mrs. Cardiff nodded at the principal and got to their feet. All three women walked into the main office and then out into the central hallway just as the first buses pulled up at the curb out front.

The school day had begun.

CHAPTER 19

TROUBLE
IN TWINSVILLE

Ray timed his morning walk perfectly, and on Wednesday he got to school just as the first buses arrived. He went through the front doors with a big crowd of kids, then walked straight across the central hallway and stopped against the far wall, scanning for faces amid the flow of kids. He was looking for Melissa. Or for James. He saw Sean, but he didn't really want to talk with him. He wanted to talk to the kids who knew who he was. The ones who knew that he was Ray. And he didn't spot either of them.

So he eased back into the heavy foot traffic, turned right, and shuffled along toward the sixth-grade hall. He was going to get to homeroom earlier than usual, but he still had some issues with the math homework, so the extra time would be good.

• • •

As the first busloads of kids came inside on Wednesday, Mrs. Cardiff stood next to the open doorway of her office, watching. She had an excellent memory for faces, and almost immediately she saw Jay Grayson walk in the door—a perfect match with the fifth-grade school picture in his student folder. Except this morning, the boy had a fresh bruise on his right cheekbone. Plus a small scrape on his chin. The nurse made a mental note of those physical issues.

The child seemed hesitant, as if he wasn't sure which way to go. And he wasn't walking with friends, wasn't talking with anyone, acted like he didn't see the three or four girls who smiled his way. He stood alone near the wall for about twenty seconds, looking this way and that, and then turned and walked toward the sixth-grade hall. *Seems like sort of a loner*, she thought. *Maybe he feels a little lost without his twin.*

Ray sat down in homeroom and started talking with Alex Grellman. He was a math whiz, and Ray needed help. He'd had some trouble with the homework about factoring—which was Jay's fault, for taking such lousy notes. Which was because all during math class on Tuesday, Jay had kept getting distracted by that girl he thought was so special—Julie Parkman.

But Ray didn't want to think about Jay. He was glad to be nowhere near his brother . . . *the nasty little rat*, he thought. *And if I never see him again in my whole life? That would be just fine.*

And Ray felt that way because the previous night had not been a happy time in Twinsville.

The problems had begun after dinner on Tuesday, when Ray and Jay had gone to their room to do homework. They sat at their double-wide desk, passing their one math book back and forth, trying to figure out the assignment. It was slow going.

After about ten minutes of struggling to explain factoring to Ray, Jay said, "Listen, forget about this stuff for a minute. I've got to tell you something."

Ray stopped chewing the end of his pencil and said, "So tell me."

Jay took a deep breath and said, "James found out. About you and me. That we're twins, and that we've been switching off at school."

Ray stared at his brother. "You're kidding, right?"

Jay shook his head. "James has twin brothers, fourth graders. And he can always tell them apart.

And when we were doing our laps at soccer practice this afternoon? He said he could tell that we
were different. He just knew. Especially since you
didn't tell me that you had a scrape on your knee
from yesterday. So he took one look at my knee
today, then looked at the way I run, and he—"

"The way you run?" Ray said. "What's that
mean?"

"Well, he watched you running on Monday,"
Jay said, "and you're slower. Plus your elbows stick
out like chicken wings."

"No, they don't—*chicken wings*? James said that?"

Jay said, "Yeah, but not making fun, just
describing. So anyway, he knows now. But he's not
gonna tell anyone. Because he—"

"I'm *slower*?" Ray said. "He thinks *I* run slower
than you do? He's crazy."

Jay said, "So . . . you're okay with it? That he
knows about us?"

Ray shrugged. "Sure. I mean, it doesn't really
matter. Everyone's gonna know on Friday anyway."
He paused a moment, then added, "And besides, I
told Melissa all about everything. On Monday
morning."

Jay's mouth dropped open. "You *what*?"

Ray said, "I told Melissa. On Monday. I didn't

want to tell her a million lies about why I seemed like such a complete idiot on Friday."

"So—like, today?" Jay said, "When I was in class with her, she *knew*? *Today*?"

Ray nodded, and a slow grin spread over his face. "Yeah, I called her after school, while you were at soccer. And she said some of the other girls know about us too. Because she told her friend, this girl named Caroline. And Melissa's really sorry about it and everything, but I told her it's no big deal." Ray paused, and his grin got bigger. "And hey, good news—she said you were really cute in science today, pretending to be all cool and smooth. Like me."

Jay slugged Ray on the shoulder. "*That's* for not telling me sooner." He punched Ray again on the same spot, harder. "And *that's* for thinking it's all so funny that everyone's been whispering and laughing behind my back all day. You and your stupid girl-friend. Who's about as cute as a warthog."

The insults made Ray clench his fists, and he wanted to hit back, but Jay's face looked so red and twisted with anger that it struck him as funny. So Ray started laughing.

And that's when civil war broke out, brother against brother. Jay jumped up and tackled Ray, knocking him off his chair. They both hit the floor, and someone's leg caught on the cord of the double-necked desk lamp. It went flying, and both light-bulbs popped as it crashed to the floor, plunging the bedroom into darkness.

By the time their dad had stomped up the stairs to stop the fight, Jay's shirt was ripped from shoulder to waist, his elbow was bleeding where it had smacked against the radiator, and Ray had a fist-shaped lump on his cheekbone and a fingernail scrape on his chin.

The boys got some first aid and a second round of scolding from their mom, then they cleaned up the mess, vacuumed the broken glass, replaced the lightbulbs, and went back to their homework. In icy silence.

Their anger chilled to become resentment, and the deep freeze continued the rest of the night. Even at breakfast on Wednesday morning, their mom said, "Boys, don't be like this. I don't know what you're fighting about, but you need to let it go and move on. I want you to shake hands with each other, right now."

So the twins shook hands, but each tried to catch the other's hand to give it a knuckle grind, and each of them squeezed extra hard, and they

held the grip so long that their dad said, "All right, knock it off, both of you. Now!"

So as Ray sat in homeroom on Wednesday, trying to understand what Alex explained about the factoring problems, not having a twin brother at all would have been just fine with him.

After the pledge, the intercom speaker crackled to life, and a voice said, "Mrs. Lane?"

"Yes?" she answered, shushing the room with her hands and eyes.

"Please send Jay Grayson to the nurse's office right away for a hearing test."

"All right."

"Thank you." And the speaker went dead.

Mrs. Lane said, "Jay, you should take your things with you. And don't worry, all the new students get their ears tested every fall. Do you know where the nurse's office is?"

Ray was on his feet already, his book bag on his shoulder. "Next to the main office?"

Mrs. Lane nodded, "That's right."

And Ray was out the door and on his way, a happy bounce in his step.

Ray normally didn't like going to the nurse's office. But this? This was great. Because if he played it right, he might be able to miss the first half of math class. No factoring, and no having to pretend to be nice to that dumb Parkman girl. For his stupid brother. On this particular morning, a trip to the nurse was going to be the *perfect* way to start the day.

CHAPTER 20

GAME OVER

Ray stood in the open doorway a second, sniffing. He had learned that it was always good to sample the air quality before entering a nurse's office. And after inhaling a few times, he decided the place smelled okay. No throw-up smells, no bathroom odors, only a faint whiff of rubbing alcohol and soap.

So Ray knocked on the door, and instantly the nurse said, "Come right in."

She was sitting at her desk on his right, and she had a laptop computer open in front of her. She turned her head, smiled, and said, "Good morning. You're Jay?" As he nodded, she said, "I'm Mrs. Cardiff." She pointed at a chair directly behind hers and said, "Please, take a seat. I'll just be a moment."

So Ray slipped his book bag off his shoulder and sat down.

He looked to his left at a poster about proper nutrition. Nothing of interest there. He looked to his right at a poster about correct posture, and immediately sat up taller in his chair. Then, glancing straight ahead at the back of the nurse's head, his eyes dropped down to where her left arm rested on her desk. And there on her desk, beside the laptop, Ray saw something. His eyes popped wide, his heart seemed to stop, and his mind went blank with a sharp jolt of electric fear. It was a bright blue folder. The double-thick student file Jay had described to him, the folder Jay had seen in Mrs. Lane's room on his second day of school. Sitting right there, right now, four feet in front of him.

Ray panicked, wanted to leap up and run out of the nurse's office, run out of the school, run all the way home. But he sat there, trying to think.

The blue folder. On the nurse's desk—what does it mean?

Has she studied it? Discovered the truth?

But if she knows, why is she acting like everything's fine?

Ray barely had his thoughts under control as the nurse spun her chair around to face him.

"All right, then," she said. She held a pair of large earphones, and the cord was plugged into the computer. "First I want to adjust the levels on the testing program. We have a specialist who comes and checks over my results, so I have to make sure I do this right. The computer does most of the work. But I have to set it correctly. I love computers these days, don't you? How they can do almost anything? Why, when I first became a school nurse, the hearing tester was almost as big as a washing machine."

Mrs. Cardiff wasn't usually this chatty, but she wanted time to get a good look at Jay Grayson. The boy seemed agitated, as if he was afraid of something.

She handed him the earphones and said, "Here, put these on—that's right, just like earmuffs. Now, let me wiggle them a little."

As she leaned forward and adjusted the headphones to fit tightly around his ears, Mrs. Cardiff could see that bruise on his cheekbone clearly. And from experience, she knew what she was seeing. Those were knuckle marks on the boy's face. Only knuckles left marks like that. Not good.

The nurse pointed and said, "That bruise on your face, does it hurt?"

"What?" Ray said. He pulled the headphones off his right ear.

The nurse said, "Does that bruise on your face hurt? How'd that happen?"

"No, it's fine. I . . . I banged it against my bed. On the board at the end. Because I slipped. On a rug."

"Hmm, I see," said the nurse, but she thought, *That's a lie.* And she was right. She said, "Does anyone in your family have hearing problems? Your mom? Your dad?"

Ray shook his head.

The nurse made a quick decision. Because a boy who feels like he has to lie about a bruise on his face could be in real danger, and his missing brother might be in danger too. It was time to be direct, to get to the heart of this case.

She said, "How about your brother? Does he have any hearing problems?"

Ray tilted his head, not sure if he had heard the question right.

The nurse reached over and took the headphones off. "I said, does your *brother* have any hearing problems?"

"M–my brother?" Ray stammered.

"Yes, Jay," the nurse said, looking straight into his eyes. "Your twin brother, Ray."

Ray stared back at the nurse, and he said the first

thing that popped into his mind. "I don't have a brother named Ray."

Which was true.

But looking into the nurse's face, Ray knew that the game was over. It was time for the truth. The whole truth.

He took a deep breath and said, "My brother's name is Jay. Because I'm Ray, not Jay. I'm Ray."

The nurse went along with him. She nodded, but she didn't know what to believe. Still, she was getting answers, so she asked another question. "And where has your brother Jay been for the past week?"

"Here at school," Ray said, "but not every day—like, not today. We've been taking turns. Today's his day to stay home."

"And your parents?" she asked.

Ray shook his head. "They don't know about it. About us staying home and stuff. They're both at work all day."

The nurse stood up. "Stay right here . . . Ray. In that chair. I'll be back in a minute." The nurse laid the headphones on her desk and hurried out of the room.

Ray didn't even turn his head to watch her leave. He knew where she was going. She had to be going to the office. To get the principal. That would have to be next. The principal.

But Ray wasn't worried. Because this was the endgame, and for the past five nights, just before falling asleep, Ray had been thinking about how this whole mess was going to be settled. He had worked out all the possible endings, so he felt ready.

And now that the final steps were beginning, Ray felt a warm wave of relief wash through his mind. It would all be over quickly now, and soon life would be so much simpler. Maybe a little more ordinary. But ordinary was okay. Ordinary sounded good—even with the twin thing revved up into overdrive.

And there really wasn't anything to worry about now. Because from this point on, right to the very end, Ray felt sure he had figured out all the possible twists and turns, every last one of them. No more surprises.

But that wasn't quite true.

CHAPTER 21

THE END BEGINS

When the nurse came back to her office, so did the principal. And Ray wasn't surprised. It only took him about four minutes to explain everything to Mrs. Lonsdale. It was very simple, really: Jay noticed there wasn't a folder for Ray, and the two of them decided they really wanted to see what it would be like to go to school without an identical twin being there.

The principal said, "Well, I hope you realize that what you've been doing is very wrong. Even dangerous. With your parents thinking both of you are safe at school, and the school not knowing anything at all about the other twin? That's not good. You and your brother have gotten yourselves off to a very bad start here at Taft Elementary School."

Ray nodded. No surprises yet. Right from the start, he and Jay had had a clear idea about all the trouble heading their way. And they both knew there would also be some punishment involved. Guaranteed.

The principal went on. "Now, Jay—I mean, Ray—I've just spoken with your mother at her office, and she has given permission for Mrs. Cardiff and me to drive you home. We'll meet your parents there in about fifteen minutes. And your brother, too. We all need to have a serious talk about this. Do you have anything else you want to say to us right now?"

Ray shook his head. "Only . . . that I'm sorry." Which was true. Because the actual size of the problem he and his brother had caused was beginning to hit him. And untangling everything wasn't going to be as simple as he'd thought it would be. Especially with Jay acting so pigheaded all of a sudden.

Still, as Ray went out to the faculty parking lot, walking between Mrs. Lonsdale and Mrs. Cardiff like a prisoner between two deputies, he couldn't help thinking, *Well, at least I won't have to deal with math class today.*

CHAPTER 22

MISSING

R ay saw the minivan in the driveway when the principal's car turned onto his street, saw his mom and dad standing in the driveway. Waiting. For him. And as they got closer, he could see their faces.

Ray gulped. This part was not going to be fun.

Still, it was going to be good to get the worst parts over with all at once. *Sort of like taking a bandage off a scraped knee,* Ray told himself. *One quick pull.*

The principal parked her car behind the minivan, got out, and walked over and introduced herself to Ray's parents. "I'm sorry this isn't a happier occasion for our first introductions," she said, "but it's always good to get a bad situation out in the open. This is Mrs. Cardiff, the school nurse."

Mrs. Grayson said, "Well, my husband and I

want to thank both of you for your help with this. Let's go inside and sit down, shall we?"

During this little conversation, Ray just stood there, not quite in the circle of grown-ups. No one looked at him, no one mentioned him. He'd have felt better even if his mom or dad had frowned at him. But it was as if he wasn't there.

He followed his mom and dad in through the kitchen door, and as the principal and nurse followed, Mrs. Grayson called out, her voice sharp and strong. "Jay? Come here to the kitchen, right this minute."

Ray didn't hear the TV on in the living room, so he walked in and put his hand on the set. It wasn't warm. *I bet he just went back to bed after I left for school*, he thought.

So he called to the kitchen, "I think he's asleep, Mom. I'll go wake him up."

But when Ray got to their room, both beds were still made, just like they'd left them before school.

Ray hurried back downstairs, and to answer the question he saw on his mom's face, he said, "Jay must be out in our hiding place."

With the grown-ups following, Ray led the way to the garage and called out, "Hey, Jay—

everyone's here. And everyone knows now. You can come out."

Nothing.

Ray said, "Maybe he fell asleep in there." He didn't really believe that, but he moved the box hiding the entry anyway and crawled in. As he did, Mr. Grayson lifted off a couple of the top boxes, and Ray looked up to see all four grown-ups peering down into the cardboard cave. And for half a second, Ray thought he saw a smile on his dad's face, just a tiny one. But he looked around at the frowning faces, shrugged, and said, "Not here."

His mom said, "Well, where is he, Ray? This isn't funny anymore. Where did he go?" Her voice was tight and shrill.

Again Ray had to shrug. "I don't know, Mom. Honest. He was still pretty mad this morning. From our fight last night. But I know Jay wouldn't do anything stupid. Or dangerous."

And the moment he'd said that, Ray wished he hadn't. Because the look of pure fear on his mom's face was like nothing he had ever seen before. And everyone else stiffened, almost stopped breathing.

There was a moment of complete silence in the garage, as though time itself had stopped and wouldn't dare take one tick forward.

And in that silence, a cell phone rang, a loud, bouncy Latin beat. Mrs. Lonsdale's face went from pale to slightly red, and she said, "That's my phone. Excuse me." And she stepped out the garage door onto the driveway.

Ray started climbing over the boxes, and his mom stretched out her hand to steady him.

As he stepped down, he said, "I mean, maybe Jay took a bus to the zoo. Or to the Rock and Roll Hall of Fame. We've been talking about that. Or he might just be at the park or something." But as he talked, Ray realized that he was just making it more and more obvious that Jay could be anywhere.

And as he stood there on the floor next to his mom, she pulled him close in a sudden, fierce hug that caught Ray completely off guard.

As Mrs. Grayson held her son so tightly that he could barely breathe, the principal put her head back in the door of the garage and said, "Jay's all right—he's been found."

CHAPTER 23

GONE

Ray had been right about Jay, about how mad he was.

Jay had been so angry that he'd hardly been able to swallow his orange juice at breakfast. He had left the house when Ray did, and on the way out he hadn't smiled once, or even said good-bye to his mom or dad. And as Ray headed off for school, Jay had snuck around to the garage, as usual.

But today Jay hated waiting in the cardboard hideout, and he sat in the dark on the rickety lawn chair in a fuming rage, furious at everyone.

Jay was angry at Ray for telling Melissa, and then not telling him that she knew. The two of them had had a good laugh about him pretending to be like Ray. They had let him make a complete fool of himself.

And he was ready to punch Melissa in the nose

for blabbing the secret to all her friends. So they could make fun of him together.

And he was mad at his mom and dad for giving him and Ray names that were almost the same. Because that wasn't a help. Ever.

Jay was angry at the whole stinking universe for setting things up so that he had to have a twin brother at all. It was so unfair, to always be compared with someone else—and it would probably be that way for the rest of his life.

But mostly, Jay was angry at himself. Because he was to blame for this mess, all of it. It had been his idea, and he was the one who had pushed Ray into taking turns going to school in the first place.

And now it had blown up in his face. Completely.

This so-called experiment that was supposed to make Ray and him feel free from each other, free from the endless comparisons? Total failure. They were supposed to have been free to just be themselves. *Yeah, right,* Jay sneered to himself as he sat stewing in the hideout. *Like that could ever happen.*

The experiment had failed miserably. Instead of feeling free, they were both locked into a prison of lies. Instead of getting to be themselves, they kept having to pretend to be more and more like each other.

And that could never work. Jay saw that now. It was stupid to have thought that they could even pretend to be the same person. They were two totally different people, always had been, always would be—no matter how it might look to others. Jay was fed up with everything—his brother, his parents, school—and girls? With Melissa laughing and jabbering to all her friends, he could forget about Julie Parkman. Or any other girl in this town.

So after his parents left for work, Jay stomped back into the house. He went up to his room and stuffed some things into his backpack, along with the lunch his mom had made for him—some money, his Cubs hat, an extra T-shirt, an extra pair of socks.

Then he went downstairs and back through the living room, turning off the lights as he went. Jay walked out the kitchen door, slamming it behind him.

And he didn't look back.

CHAPTER 24

THE REAL
JAY GRAYSON

When he left home on that warm Wednesday morning in September, did Jay Grayson head for the bus station in downtown Cleveland? Did he start walking toward Interstate 480 so he could hitch a ride somewhere, anywhere? Or did he set out walking straight west, just hiking toward his grandparents' farm in Indiana?

Standing at the end of his driveway with his backpack on, all those ideas certainly ran through his mind.

But Jay had already chosen a different destination.

Eleven and a half minutes later, Jay checked himself in at the office of Taft Elementary School. And when the secretary gave him a confused look and asked him his name, he said, "Jay Grayson."

Because that's who he was. The real Jay Grayson. And the real Jay Grayson was given an unexcused tardy slip to take to his first-period teacher.

So Jay went to math class.

Walking toward Mrs. Pell's room, Jay knew what he was going to do. Because he was going to walk right into that room, walk right over to where Ray was sitting, and in a voice loud enough for everyone to hear, he was going to say, "My name is Jay Grayson, and you're sitting in my seat. So move it. Now."

Because Jay was ready for the big scene. In front of Julie. In front of everyone. And all the kids would be amazed to see both of them, identical twins. Even the kids who already knew were going to be amazed. There would be a burst of confusion. And then the principal would be called in. And that would be the end of it, the end of the pretending. And whatever happened after that? Jay didn't care. Not one bit. Let it happen.

So it was a huge disappointment for Jay when he arrived at math class and discovered that his seat was empty—no Ray. He gave Mrs. Pell his tardy slip and sat down, and thirty seconds later the teacher asked him to go to the chalkboard and demonstrate how to find the greatest common factor of 128 and

42. So Jay had no choice but to jump into the stream of the math class and go with the flow.

But when Ray came back to math from wherever he was at the moment? *Then* there was going to be a scene. The big one. And Jay was ready.

Except Jay didn't know that as he was leaving home to walk to school, Ray and Mrs. Cardiff and Mrs. Lonsdale were getting into a car in the school parking lot.

And Jay also did not know that two minutes after he had checked in tardy at the office, the school secretary had phoned the principal, and in a puzzled tone of voice said, "Mrs. Lonsdale? I'm sorry to interrupt you, but that boy you and Mrs. Cardiff just drove away with? He's back here at school, right now. And—and I just wanted you to know that."

And that phone call was why the principal and the school nurse walked back into the school ten minutes after Jay did, followed by Mr. and Mrs. Grayson and their son Ray.

And two minutes after that, the intercom speaker in the sixth-grade math room hummed and then crackled with static, and the school secretary's voice said, "Mrs. Pell?"

"Yes?"

"Please send Jay Grayson to the office right away."

And one and a half minutes later, when Jay appeared at the desk in the main office, the secretary looked at him, then squinted, and looked again. And then she pointed toward the door of the principal's office and said, "Go right in."

So Jay opened the door and went in.

CHAPTER 25

DISCORD, UNISON, HARMONY

The principal's office was small. As Jay arrived, the population of the little room rose to six: two school people, two parents, and a pair of twins. There were chairs for everyone, and the extra furniture made the room feel that much smaller.

Jay sat in the only empty seat, right next to Ray, and as he did, he glanced sideways. He knew from the look on his brother's face that things had already been unpleasant. Their chairs were jammed together, so as they sat there, straight and still, Jay's right arm was touching Ray's left. And immediately Ray gave him a tiny nudge. Jay replied by flexing a muscle, a signal so small that no one else knew it happened. But the twins had opened a line of communication. Jay's anger was still fresh in his mind, but this was bigger than that. They were in this thing together, and their contact gave each of them some comfort. Which did not last long.

The principal cleared her throat and looked around quickly from face to face. "Well, now that we're all here, I'd like to begin by saying that Mrs. Cardiff and I and the whole staff at Taft Elementary School are very distressed that this situation has . . . happened. I've been principal here for nine years, and I taught math here for seven years before that, and we've never had anything like this . . . happen. Before."

Mrs. Cardiff quickly added, "Of course, we're very glad that this situation hasn't resulted in any mishaps to either of your sons, because that's our first concern, always. We want every child to be safe and cared for. And supervised. And we take that responsibility very seriously."

The principal nodded at the nurse's comments and went on. "Now, of course, we'll need to contact the school your sons attended in Colorado to be certain that the student files they sent here were complete. Because the way the information was transmitted to us was confusing, to say the least. And our school district will be reviewing all of our new student registration procedures to be certain that nothing like this can ever happen again."

Mrs. Lonsdale stopped and cleared her throat, and after glancing at Ray and Jay, she said, "And, we'll also have to determine the appropriate . . . consequences. For the boys. For skipping several days of school. And that will be settled after I talk to the superintendent. Because we may be looking at a suspension . . . or rather, suspensions."

As the principal said that word, Jay and Ray felt a tremor as each of them flinched. A suspension was a bad thing. A blot on a school record. Permanent.

"You plan to talk to the superintendent?" Mr. Grayson asked. "Because won't that sort of be making this whole thing public? Wouldn't it make just as much sense to handle this yourself, right here at the school?"

The principal said, "We've had a serious incident here, so the consequences need to be serious as well. That just stands to reason."

Mrs. Grayson nodded and said, "We agree, Mrs. Lonsdale, but I think I can explain what my husband means. You see, we both work for an insurance company. I'm a claims analyst—looking at situations, determining if there might have been any fraud, any dishonesty, anything unusual. And my husband is a claims adjuster, the person who goes out and talks with the people involved. He's sort of an investigator. So I think he's asking if there's a way to keep this from becoming more difficult than it already is."

Mr. Grayson nodded. "Because, I mean, can't you imagine the headlines in the local newspaper? 'School Loses Sixth Grader for a Week'—that couldn't be good, not for the school or for our family."

Jay felt a definite nudge from Ray, then a steady pressure against his arm as their dad kept talking. And Jay nudged back. And those nudges meant, *Are you hearing what I'm hearing? Because it sounds like Dad is on the attack—defending us!*

Turning toward the nurse, Mr. Grayson went on, "You mentioned that you're glad neither of the boys had a mishap. My wife and I are glad about that too. We're very glad the boys are safe, and we're also glad that no lawyers need to get involved. In this situation."

The principal narrowed her eyes and said, "I'm still not sure I understand exactly what you're saying, Mr. Grayson."

Jay wasn't sure either. And neither was Ray.

Because the boys had never heard their parents talking to other grown-ups so seriously. Or maybe they just hadn't listened much before. But they were certainly listening now, each of them sitting still, barely breathing. Except now, they were practically elbowing each other to punctuate the points being made by both sides. Because it was clear that there were sides now. This was starting to feel like a battle.

Mr. Grayson looked the principal straight in the eye and said, "What I'm saying is, that I am hoping that you will leave the disciplinary consequences for our boys up to their mother and me. They lied and they skipped school—both bad things, and they will be punished. At home. I can guarantee that. But here at school, I really think it would be best for our sons if they could simply get on with their work. To get past this . . . incident. Quickly. Starting today."

The principal frowned and said, "But they've broken so many rules that—"

Mr. Grayson interrupted, "Yes, but as I see it, Ray and Jay's previous school did send your school information about each boy, two files—correct?" Mrs. Lonsdale nodded, and Mr. Grayson said, "And your school lost one of those files by mistake. One student, lost—correct?" Again the principal nodded. And sounding more and more like a prosecutor in a courtroom, Mr. Grayson said, "It was certainly wrong for the boys to take advantage of that. However—and this is my main point—it was the school's mistake that allowed this situation to develop in the first place. Someone might even call the school's mistake negligence. But negligence is such an unpleasant term. A legal term. So I think we should just call this whole thing a mistake, and move on."

Jay raised his hand.

All eyes turned to him, and the nurse said, "Yes, Ray?"

And Jay said, "I'm Jay."

And the nurse said, "Right—sorry. Ray's the one with the bruise on his face. Do you have something to add, Jay?" Mrs. Cardiff was glad for this interruption, because the exchange between Mr. Grayson and the principal was getting a bit too heated, and by the look in Mrs. Lonsdale's eye, it was about to burst into flames.

Jay was feeling the heat too, feeling responsible for this giant mess. He nodded at the nurse. "I just want to say that this was all my idea. I wanted to see what it would be like to be at school without being a twin for a while. And I'm really sorry. The whole thing was my idea—so I'm the one who should be in trouble."

Ray shook his head and said, "I went along with all of it. So it's my fault too. And I'm just as sorry as you are. And I should get punished just as much too. So stop trying to make everything be all about you, okay?"

And instantly, instinctively, Jay hauled back and punched Ray on the shoulder. Hard.

Which made the nurse gasp.

And which made Mrs. Grayson shout, "Jay! You stop that!"

But all the anger Jay had been feeling just a half hour earlier came rushing back, and he blurted out, "You don't even know if I'm Jay or not, Mom. Nobody does. Except him," he said, jerking his thumb at Ray. "And nobody cares who we really are, either one of us. We're just 'the twins.' And I'm sick of it."

Mrs. Grayson's eyes brimmed with tears. "Why, of course we care who you are, sweetheart, both of you. And we know who you are . . . we do."

"Oh yeah?" Jay snapped. "When I stayed home last Thursday, did you know it was me and not Ray? No. And when we went to the mall on Friday, I was wearing Ray's sweatshirt and sunglasses and hat. That was me. And you never knew a thing. And if Ray hadn't goofed up on Saturday, *I* would have gone skating too, and you never would have guessed it was me. You *never* know who we are for sure, either of you—unless you do the freckle-check."

Mrs. Cardiff said, "The freckle-check?"

Mr. Grayson nodded. "Ray's got a freckle on his right ankle."

And Mrs. Cardiff made a mental note of that possibly useful bit of information.

The small office got quiet as Mrs. Grayson dabbed at her eyes with the tissue the principal handed her. And the angry feelings the adults had been starting to express began to drain out of the room, replaced by concern for these boys. And also curiosity.

Because this glimpse into the land of twins was completely new for Mrs. Cardiff and Mrs. Lonsdale. And Ray and Jay's parents were getting some fresh views as well.

Mrs. Cardiff felt it was time to step in as a mediator, one of her strong points. She smiled at Jay and then Ray. "What I'm hearing is that what you two did was a way to deal with this problem of being constantly mistaken for each other, of feeling like you're always overshadowed by each other. Is that right?"

Both boys nodded, and Jay said, "Yeah, like, forever."

"But you both see that the way you chose to behave wasn't helpful, or honest? Right?" the nurse asked.

Again both boys nodded.

Mrs. Cardiff continued, "Well, this problem isn't really going to go away, no matter what *we* do. It's something each of you have to learn to deal with as best you can. You can see that, right? I'm sure you can. But there might be some ways the school could help. Can you think of any?"

Jay spoke up immediately. "Could I be in a different homeroom?"

And Ray nodded. "Yeah. That would be good."

The principal said, "We can make that happen right away. And I don't see why we can't try to put you into as many different classes as possible. How about that?"

More nodding, with the parents joining in as well.

Mrs. Cardiff paused, because she really wanted to get this next part right. And she didn't want to sound like a nurse, or a teacher, or even like a parent. She wanted to sound like a friend. She looked into each face and said, "But you know, boys, if this problem is going to get better, most of the work is going to be yours, not ours. We can help, but you have to be patient with us and help us. Because I'm sure you're not the same. No two people ever are. You have to let us get to know you. Can you do that? And try to be more patient with each other, too?"

Ray and Jay looked at each other, and a signal no one else could see passed between them. And they both turned to the nurse, nodded, and said, "Yes." In perfect unison.

The principal turned to Mr. and Mrs. Grayson and said, "I think your ideas about how to handle this problem are just right. To help the boys move ahead with their schoolwork. And I thank you both for your understanding. About our mistake."

Both parents nodded and smiled, and Mrs. Grayson said, "And thank you, too. We're not trying to be difficult, honestly. We just want what's best for the twins—I mean, for Jay and Ray."

And Mrs. Lonsdale nodded back and said, "Exactly what we want as well."

All the grown-ups were suddenly on their best behavior. It felt like the sun had come out after a big thunderstorm. And the boys picked up on that. Ray sneaked a quick look at Jay, who was sneaking a quick look at him, and each saw relief on the other's face. And both looked away quickly, because this would have been the wrong time for a smile. But for the moment, the worst was over, and they knew it.

The next ten minutes were a flurry of activity as the principal consulted with the school secretary to separate the twins as much as possible during the school day.

Since Jay was the name already connected with a face in Mrs. Lane's homeroom, it made sense for Jay to stay put, and Ray would be the one who moved to Mrs. Abbot's homeroom.

In fact, for that same reason, Jay's schedule stayed as it was, and Ray was given a whole different one—which Ray didn't like at first, because that meant Jay would remain Melissa's lab partner. But he let it slide. Besides, there were sure to be some nice girls in the other classes too. And Ray actually thought he got the better deal, because it was like he was going to get a brand-new start. As himself. As Ray Grayson. His new locker was at the far end of the sixth-grade hall. Plus, he would never have to pretend he liked playing soccer again for as long as he lived.

As it ended up, the only class the boys were going to have together was gym. They would also be together during sixth-grade lunch, but they wouldn't have to sit anywhere near each other. Unless they chose to.

And the social studies report that was due in class today? Jay would turn it in, because he'd done most of the work on it. And Ray would have an extra week to finish one of his own.

When their schedules were set, Mrs. Lonsdale said, "Jay, you're going from here right to social studies, and this is a note to get you into class late."

Turning to Ray, she said, "You're going to the art room, Ray. And here's a note to explain to Ms. Chu that you are now in that class, and this is a copy of your new schedule—you'll also need to get textbooks from all your teachers." She paused and looked from face to face. "So now it's up to you. And I do not want to hear anything but good news about either of you boys for the rest of the year, is that understood?"

Both boys nodded and said, "Yes, Mrs. Lonsdale." In unison.

Before they left the office, Ray and Jay each got a long hug from their mom. Who almost got weepy again.

And each son also got a strong handshake and a short hug from their dad. Who did *not* almost get weepy. At all. And from the look in his eye, Jay and Ray knew that their father hadn't been kidding about what he'd said to the principal during the meeting. About the consequences they would face. At home.

But that would be much later. It would be hours and hours before they would have to deal with their dad again. So the immediate threat level dropped away to almost zero.

The boys left the office together, and when they were about ten feet down the hall, Ray looked back over his shoulder.

And Jay said, "Anybody following us?"

Ray said, "Nope. Mom's watching, but we're on our own. Clean getaway."

Jay said, "Sweet."

The brothers walked side by side in silence until they reached the corner where the hallways crossed. They stopped, then looked at each other for a second or two. It didn't feel like looking into a mirror, not at all. And they both grinned.

"Amazing week, huh?" Ray said.

Jay nodded. "Definitely. Hey, I think Julie Parkman's gonna be in your art class now. Say hi to her for me, okay?"

Ray smiled. "You can count on it. And when you see Melissa this afternoon, just be yourself, okay? She thinks you're cute. In a dorky sort of way."

Jay resisted the urge to punch his brother, then laughed. "Cute but dorky. I can live with that. So listen, have a good one, okay? And maybe I'll see you at lunch."

Ray nodded. "Yeah. Maybe so."

Jay turned and walked down the main hallway toward social studies, and Ray headed toward the art room.

After walking in opposite directions for about fifteen seconds, they each took a look back over their shoulders. In unison.

And they both smiled, nodded, and kept walking.

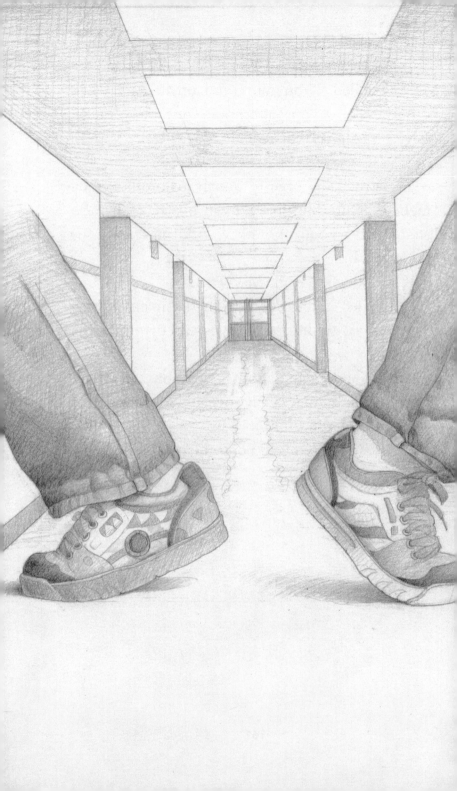